Calligraphy Lesson is the first English-language collection of short stories by Mikhail Shishkin, the most acclaimed contemporary author in Russia. Spanning his entire writing career, [illegible] "Calligraphy Lesson," which heralded an entirely [illegible] erature and won him Russia's prestigio[illegible] essays reflecting on the transcendent in[illegible] st story, "Nabokov's Inkblot," written in 2[illegible] eater in Zurich. A master prose writer and unique stylist, Shishkin is [illegible] greatest Russian writers, such as Tolstoy, Bunin, and Pasternak, and is the living embodiment of the combination of style and content that has made Russian literature so unique and universally popular for over two centuries. Shishkin's breathtakingly beautiful writing style comes across perfectly in these stories, where he experiments with the forms and ideas that are worked into his grand novels while exploring entirely new literary territory in the space between fiction and creative nonfiction as he reflects on the most important and universal themes in life: love, happiness, art, death, resurrection...

More praise for Mikhail Shishkin:

"Often sings with powerfully estranged, original observations... minutiae and grand philosophy collide on every page."—BORIS FISHMAN, *The New York Times Book Review*

"Shishkin is interested in what is most precious and singular in classic Russian fiction: the passionate inquiry into what, in *Maidenhair*, is called the 'soul, quintessence, pollen.'" —SAM SACKS, *The Wall Street Journal*

"Mikhail Shishkin is the Ian McEwan of Russia. A prize-winning writer who enjoys stunning commercial and critical success...His latest novel [*The Light and the Dark*]...is striking proof that great Russian literature didn't die with Dostoevsky." —*Monocle Magazine*

"[Shishkin] manages to engage Russia's literary heritage while at the same time creating something new and altogether original." —*World Literature Today*

"Shishkin has been described as the heir apparent of the great Russian novelists, and indeed, there are times when he seems to have taken the best from each of them." —*The Quarterly Conversation*

"As an extraordinary prose stylist, Shishkin has license to be unconventional... *Maidenhair* is likely a work of genius."—*World Literature Today*

CALLIGRAPHY LESSON

CALLIGRAPHY LESSON

Mikhail Shishkin

TRANSLATED FROM THE RUSSIAN BY
MARIAN SCHWARTZ, LEO SHTUTIN,
SYLVIA MAIZELL, AND
MARIYA BASHKATOVA

DEEP VELLUM PUBLISHING
DALLAS, TEXAS

Deep Vellum Publishing
2919 Commerce St. #159, Dallas, Texas 75226
deepvellum.org · @deepvellum

Some stories were published previously:
"The Half-Belt Overcoat" in *Read Russia: An Anthology of New Voices* (May 2012)
"Calligraphy Lesson" in Words Without Borders (July 2007)
"Nabokov's Inkblot" in New England Review (Volume 34, Nos. 3–4, 2014)
"Of Saucepans and Star-Showers" in Spolia (March 2013)
"In a Boat Scratched on a Wall" originally appeared in slightly different form as
"Mikhail Shishkin: A revolution for Russia's words" in the *Independent* (March 22, 2013)

ISBN: 978-1-941920-03-9 (paperback) · 978-1-941920-02-2 (ebook)
LIBRARY OF CONGRESS CONTROL NUMBER: 2015935163

—

Издание осуществлено при участии Программы поддержки переводов русской литературы TRANSCRIPT Фонда Михаила Прохорова.

The publication of this book was made possible with the support of the Mikhail Prokhorov Foundation's Transcript program to support the translation of Russian literature.

—

Cover design & typesetting by Anna Zylicz · annazylicz.com

Text set in Bembo, a typeface modeled on typefaces cut by Francesco Griffo for Aldo Manuzio's printing of *De Aetna* in 1495 in Venice.

Deep Vellum titles are published under the fiscal sponsorship of The Writer's Garret, a nationally recognized nonprofit literary arts organization.

Distributed by Consortium Book Sales & Distribution.
Printed in the United States of America on acid-free paper.

Contents

The Half-Belt Overcoat

There's a famous police photograph of Robert Walser, taken at the place of his death: winter, a white incline, tracks in deep snow, a man fallen supine, arms outstretched. His old man's hat flung to the side. That's how he was found by children on their Christmas walk.

He described his own death in a story published half a century before his final Christmas. The protagonist of this brief little tale is a lost soul, inconspicuous, needed by no one—and yet, to make things worse, also a genius and master of the world. He wearies of being unneeded and escapes from his troubles like this: he buries the world in a snowstorm and lays himself down in a drift.

Foreknowledge of one's own death is not, however, the privilege of the writer. It's just that it's easy to catch him red-handed—in the literal sense: the hand records whatever is revealed to him at a particular juncture. Such breakthroughs happen in every person's life. Holes in matter. Points of transmission. In such moments the composer comes by his melody, the poet his lines, the lover his love, the prophet his God.

In that instant you encounter what everyday existence holds asunder: the visible and the invisible, the worldly and the sacred.

You begin to breathe in time with a space in which all things occur simultaneously—those that have been and those yet to be.

Reality has been playing hide-and-seek with you, hiding behind the past and the future like a child who's squeezed himself in under the fur coats hanging in the hallway, and now jumps out at you, sweaty, happy, bursting with laughter: here I am! How'd you manage that—went right past and didn't see me! Now you're it!

To see your own death in such a moment is nothing, for there arises in all its glorious patency the knowledge that I was never born, but have always been. Suddenly comes the realization that there's no need to cling on to life, because I *am* life. And it is not I who can sense the smell of mulch exuding from the forest's mouth, it is the universe sniffing its own scent with my nostrils.

If you can measure your life by anything at all, it's probably by the number of such encounters allotted to you.

I remember very well how I experienced that for the first time. My twelfth year. The smell of peat bogs burning around Moscow. The hazy country mornings of seventy-two. A charred aftertaste to everything, even the hot strawberries from the garden-bed. Mum went on holiday to a rest home on the upper Volga, and took me with her. One of my first trips away.

It rained incessantly, we lived in a damp, mosquito-infested little house, and at first I was bored, nightly film screenings notwithstanding, but after a while the weather improved, we got a new canteen neighbour, Uncle Vitya, and our life took a turn for the better. We swam with him, took motorboat rides on the Volga, went on forest rambles. Sinewy and gold-toothed, Uncle Vitya made Mum laugh no end with his stories. I didn't get half of his jokes, but the way he told them made it impossible not to laugh. I took a great liking to Mum's new acquaintance. What's more, I was bowled over by the fact that he worked in a recording van—a "Tonwagen." No doubt I was already spellbound by words.

There I go, presumptuously calling that teenager myself, though I'm not at all sure whether he'd agree to acknowledge himself in me as I am now: grey-haired, advanced in life, a sickly bore with a brazenly protruding belly. He'd be very surprised: can that really be me? I don't know that I could find anything to answer. Not likely. We may be namesakes—but so what?

Among Uncle Vitya's stories I somehow remember one about how, skating on the river as a child, he and other boys would sometimes happen upon frogs frozen into the ice. If you peed on them they'd come to life and start moving. And another one about the war. He told us about the penals[1] whose only hope was to get wounded. Redeem your guilt with blood and you'd have your decorations and rank restored. And so they'd resort to self-infliction, shooting themselves in the arm or foot through a loaf of bread so there'd be no gunpowder traces in the wound.

It had never occurred to me that Mum liked to dance, but now she'd be out dancing with Uncle Vitya every evening.

One day Mum started speaking to me in a strange voice. If Uncle Vitya ever asked me about Dad, she implored, I should tell him that he was dead.

"But he's not dead," I said, surprised. "He just moved away."

She pressed my head to her breast:

"But you're my clever boy and you understand everything."

I understood nothing, but nodded all the same.

And I began waiting for Uncle Vitya to ask me about Dad.

It was strange to see Mum rouging and powdering herself, making up her eyes, painting her lips, spraying perfume on her neck, and doing her nails—I'd be hit by the sharp smell of nail varnish. I had never known her like this before.

---

1 I.e., the completely expendable members of penal battalions, which consisted primarily of convicted military personnel, Gulag inmates, and POWs.—*Trans.*

Mum was a teacher, she taught Russian language and literature, and by that time she'd already become head of School No. 59 on the Arbat. Ever since year one I'd commuted with her across the whole city—initially from Presnia, where we lived in a communal apartment, and later from Matveyevskaya, where we were given a two-room flat in a new housing development.

Naturally, she wanted to keep her child close by, at her school, but this made life much more complicated for me. Her role model was some retired maths teacher. His son had been in his class, and he knew the subject better than anyone else, but when his father called him up to the blackboard all he'd ever say was "Sit down, C"—even if his son had got the problem correct. I had to go through something similar when our class was being divided into English and German sets. I wanted to go in the English set—and with good reason, because German was a kind of punishment for those who weren't doing well: do badly, went the threat, and it'll be the German set for you. I was doing well, but Mum put me exactly where I didn't want to be. So none of the other parents could reproach her for anything. School came first for her, things personal and domestic second.

Her generation had grown up under the slogan "The Motherland is Calling!"

Perhaps, if I hadn't got into a university with a military chair after finishing school,[2] she would equally have sent me off to Afghanistan not only with sorrow but also with a sense of having fulfilled her mother's duty to the nation. I don't know. Incidentally, it would seem that I am to this day a reserve officer of the nonexistent army of that nonexistent nation. I did, after all, once swear an oath in a military camp near Kovrov

2 Enrolling in a higher-education institution with a military chair was (and remains) a way for young males to avoid otherwise compulsory military service.—*Trans.*

to defend the soon-to-disintegrate motherland till the last drop of my blood. We had to kiss the red standard, I remember, so I brought it to my lips—and got a great whiff of smoked fish. No doubt our commanders had been tucking into some beer and fish and wiping their hands on the velvet cloth.

While still at school I didn't realize, of course, how hard it must have been for Mum and all our teachers: they were faced with the insoluble problem of teaching children to tell the truth whilst initiating them into a world of lies. The written law requires that truth be told, but the unwritten dictates that if you do, you'll be facing the music later.

They taught us lies they themselves didn't believe because they loved and wanted to save us. Of course, they were afraid of wrongly spoken words, but they were afraid for us even more than they were for themselves. The country, after all, was in the grip of a deadly word game. You needed to say the right words and not say the wrong ones. The line had never been drawn, but inside everyone sensed where it lay. Our teachers were trying to save truth-loving youths from folly, to inject them with a life-giving dose of fear. You might feel a little momentary sting, but then you'd have immunity for life.

We may have been badly taught in chemistry or English, but at least we got illustrative lessons in the difficult art of survival—how to say one thing, and think and do another.

The gods of the grownups were long dead, but we had to venerate them during idolatrous rituals. School taught us children of slaves the meaning of submission. If you want to achieve anything, you have to learn how to pronounce the dead words of a dead language, in which that dead life stagnated and rotted away.

Generally, what does it mean to be a good teacher?

Clearly, a good teacher under any regime must cultivate in his pupils those qualities which will help them later in life, and will not teach them to go against the current, because they're going to need a completely different type of knowledge: the knowledge of the traffic laws in this particular life. Veer into the oncoming lane and you're heading for a crash. You need to reverse and merge into the mainstream flow. If you want to get somewhere in this life, earn a decent wage, provide for your family and children, you have to blend into the mainstream: you're the boss—I'm the fool, I'm the boss, you're the fool, honour and profit lie not in one sack, who keeps company with wolves will learn to howl.

A bad teacher, meanwhile, will instruct his charges to live by a different law, the law of the conservation of human dignity. By and large this is a road to marginalisation at best, and to jail or suicide at worst. Unless they just shoot you.

Does this mean that bad teachers were good, and good ones bad? Then again, it's always been like that in Russia: the right on the left, the left on the right. It's an age-old question, and one that still hasn't been answered: if you love your Motherland, should you wish her victory or defeat? It's still not completely clear where the Motherland ends and the regime begins, so entangled have they become.

Take hockey, for instance. On both sides of the barbed wire, USSR–Canada matches were regarded as the symbolic clash of two systems. By the end of Soviet power we were supporting the Canadians against the Soviets. But in seventy-two, the year of the epoch-making Summit Series, the teenager I obstinately refer to as myself still inhabited an unshadowed, prelapsarian world—and supported "our lads."

It really was a strange old nation. Hockey victories prolonged the regime's life, while defeats shortened it. You couldn't tell from close up that *that* Paul Henderson goal, scored from the goalmouth 34 seconds before the end of the final game, not only changed the outcome of the series, but became the point of no return for the entire world empire created by the moustachio'd despot. From that moment on, its disintegration became only a matter of time.

It's curious that a man who struck at the very heart of my country should accept his fate in an eminently Russian manner: first he turned to drink, having ditched hockey, and then became a proselytiser.

Hockey has found its way into these pages because our school happened to stand just opposite the Canadian embassy. In front of it would park incredible foreign limousines that had turned into our Starokonnyushenny Lane straight from American movies. You could press up against the window and take a good look at the dashboard—the number 220 on the speedometer was especially impressive—and we boys in our mousy-grey uniforms would heatedly debate the merits of Mustangs over Cadillacs or those of Chevrolets over Fords till a policeman leapt out of the booth outside the embassy gates and sent us packing.

A reception for the Canadian hockey players was held in the embassy. Word of the Canadians' arrival spread instantly, and we crowded on the opposite pavement, trying to get a look at our idols. These were our gods, come down from television's ice rink, and it was strange to see them in suits and ties. In the first-floor windows of the Arbat townhouse, flung open on that warm September day in seventy-two, we caught glimpses of Phil Esposito, "Bullyboy" Cashman and brothers Frank and Pete Mahovlich. In response to our adoring screams they peered out of the windows, smiled, waved, gave us thumbs up—all as if to say, Well, fellas, ain't life just dandy!

So many years have passed, yet still I can see, vividly as ever, the toothless grin of Bobby Clarke, who'd leaned out of the window and thrown us a badge. Other players, too, began throwing badges and sticks of chewing gum. Even some biscuits. It all really kicked off then!

Try as I might to catch something, anything, I was shouldered aside by those with more luck on their side. I would have ended up empty-handed. But then the miraculous happened. Bobby Clarke, who was almost lying on the windowsill, began jabbing his finger in my direction. I couldn't believe my eyes. He was looking at *me*, and threw *me* some gum. I caught it! He laughed and gave me another thumbs up—you did good, son! It was then that we were driven off by the police. I shared the gum with my friends, but the wrapper I held on to for ages. Need I mention that it was the best-tasting gum I've ever had in my life?

The next day Mum came into our class. She had her strict face on. Mum knew how to be strict, and when she was the whole school was afraid of her.

She began saying that our behaviour had brought shame and dishonour upon the school and the whole country as well. We'd been photographed by foreign correspondents, and now the whole world would see how we'd debased ourselves by fighting over their chewing gum.

Everyone was silent. I felt injustice in these accusations. And suddenly, to my own surprise, I spoke out.

"Why does our country have no chewing gum?"

"Our country doesn't have a lot of things," Mum replied. "But that doesn't mean you have to lose human dignity."

I didn't forget that.

As headmistress, Mum was the school's representative of that prison system, and she had it hard. I know she shielded and saved the skins of many. Trying to do whatever possible, she rendered unto Caesar the things which were Caesar's, and Pushkin unto the children. For several generations Pushkin was a secret code, the key to the preservation of the human in this bedevilled country. By then many already believed that the worse things were, the better, the sooner everything would go to pieces, but those like her strived to endow an inhuman existence with humanity. There was no saving her own skin, though—she got what was coming to her, and then some.

By the time I was seventeen our relationship had deteriorated to the extent that I'd stopped talking to her. Completely. We lived in the same flat but I wouldn't even say hello to her. I couldn't forgive her being a Party member, nor our having to write essays on *Virgin Lands* and *Malaya Zemlya*[3] at school. I thought that the struggle against the odious system must be waged without compromise—starting with yourself, your family, those closest to you. I wanted to live not by lies,[4] but I didn't understand then that I wasn't a hero, I was just a little brat. My silence, too, I think, shortened her life.

Now, no sooner have I written that I'd stopped talking to Mum than I sense that I've not written the whole truth, and have ended up lying as a result.

Yes, I never even said hello to her, but not only because I'd read *The Kolyma Tales* and *The Gulag Archipelago*,[5] which had inexplicably ended up in my possession around that time and changed much in my youthful conception of the world. Of course not. The conflict arose because of my first love. Mum didn't like that girl. She didn't like her at all.

At school she was the all-powerful headmistress, she could quell an inexperienced teacher's unruly class with a single glance, but at home, in her relationship with her own son, she turned out to be completely helpless. Of course the mother wished her son well. But she didn't know

---

3 The first and third installments, respectively, of Brezhnev's ghostwritten memoir trilogy, for which he was awarded the Lenin Prize for Literature in 1980.—*Trans*

4 An allusion to Solzhenitsyn's essay "Live Not by Lies" (1974), an appeal for moral courage.—*Trans.*

5 Varlam Shalamov's *The Kolyma Tales* (1978) and Solzhenitsyn's *Gulag Archipelago* (1973) are classics of Gulag literature.—*Trans.*

how to do him good. And of course Mum was totally right about that girl. But I realised that only later.

Disaster struck at Mum's school when Andropov came to power. No one knew he was already mortally ill. Once again everyone got frightened of their own fear.

The seniors wanted to organise an evening dedicated to the memory of Vysotsky. Mum's colleagues tried to dissuade her, but she authorized it. The evening went ahead. The kids sang his songs, recited his poems, listened to his recordings. Someone informed on the headmistress.

The school got an exemplary slap on the wrist to teach others a lesson.

I'd already moved out by then. I remember how I came home and Mum told me how she'd been summoned, boorishly spoken to, yelled at. She tried to defend herself, to explain. No one was going to listen to her.

She wanted to live out her life without losing human dignity. For that she got absolutely trampled.

For the first time, I think, Mum burst into tears in front of me. I didn't know what to say, I just sat beside her and stroked her on the shoulder.

Suddenly I wanted to ask her forgiveness for not having spoken to her for almost a whole year, but I never did.

Mum got kicked out of work, a blow from which she would never recover. School was her whole life.

She fell seriously ill. First her heart. Then cancer. So began the hospitals, the operations.

By then I was working at a school myself, at the no. 444 on Pervomaiskaya Street, and after lessons I'd go and see her. I spent hours in the hospital ward, doing my marking, fetching Mum something to drink, giving her the bedpan, reading her the paper, cutting her nails, just being close by. It we spoke at all, it was of trivialities. Or rather, of what seemed important then, but now, so many years on, seems unimportant.

I kept meaning to ask her forgiveness, but somehow I never managed to.

Later I described it all in *The Taking of Izmail*: her neighbour in the hospital who, bald from chemotherapy, never took off her beret, which made her look like a caricature of an artist; how bits of her nails, grown long on her gnarled toes, would fly all over the ward when I clumsily attempted to cut them; how I brought in some boards for her bed, because Mum couldn't get to sleep on its caved-in wire frame.

The novel, written a few years after Mum's death, took its rise from Russian literature, containing as it does many quotations, associations and interweaving plot threads, but by the end I was simply describing what was going on in my own life. From the complex to the simple. From the literary and the learned to Mum's foam-filled bra, which she wore after they cut off her breasts. From Old-Slavonic centos to her quiet death, which she so longed for to release her from the pain.

There were a great many people at her funeral: teachers with whom she'd worked, former pupils. She'd accumulated a lot of pupils over the years. Only through your own life can you truly teach anything of any significance.

I was stunned to see her lying in the coffin with an Orthodox chaplet on her forehead. I don't know where it came from, Mum was anything but a church person. She was a completely sincere non-believer. That's how she'd been brought up. So when I was born she didn't want me christened. And not because she feared repercussions—at the beginning of sixty-one, when Stalin still lay in the Mausoleum, she was the school's Party organiser. She just genuinely couldn't understand: what would be the point? Grandma had me christened on the sly at the church in Udelnaya, where we spent the summer at our dacha.

Even as a child, it was clear to me that church was a place for uneducated grannies, like my own, with three years of parochial school under her belt.

Later I thought that the old go to church because they fear death more than the young. And I didn't yet know that, on the contrary, it is the young who have the greater fear.

It was only after Mum passed away that I sensed acutely how essential it is for close people to engage in one all-important conversation. Usually that conversation gets put off—it isn't easy to start talking about the things that matter most over breakfast or somewhere in the metro. Something always gets in the way. I needed to ask Mum for forgiveness, but in all those years I never did manage to. When I began writing *The Taking of Izmail*, I thought it a novel about history, about the nation, about destiny, about the word, but it turned out to be that very conversation.

Most likely, such a conversation cannot take place during life in any case. It's vital that it should come about, but what matter whether it happens before or after the end? The important thing is that she heard me and forgave me.

Between operations, during the time she had away from the hospitals, Mum would sort out her lifetime's worth of photographs. She asked me to buy some albums and glued the photos into them, annotating each one with the names of the people it featured, and sometimes she'd write stories associated with these people into the margins. The result was a family archive—for the grandchildren.

After her death I took the albums over to mine. And when I was leaving for Switzerland, I left them all with my brother. The albums were stored in his house near Moscow.

The house was burnt down. All our photographs were destroyed.

All I have left is a handful of childhood snaps.

One of them, a picture of me, was taken, probably by my father, while we were still living in Presnia, though we moved to Matveyeskaya that same year. I'm in year four. I'm wearing an overcoat with a half-belt that's out of the camera's view. I remember that overcoat perfectly—it was a hand-me-down from my brother. I had to wear all his hand-me-downs. But here's why the overcoat has stuck in my mind. Mum would often tell this story. It's very short.

To get to school from Matveyevskaya we'd take the no. 77 bus to Dorogomilovskaya Street, where we changed to an Arbat-bound trolleybus, or alternatively we could take the same bus in the other direction to the railway station, and then on to Kievsky Station. That morning we went to the station. The first snow had fallen during the night. Thousands of feet had trampled the platform into a skating rink. When the train pulled in everyone dashed for the doors. You had to storm the already overflowing carriages, squeeze yourself into the jam-packed vestibules. Between the edge of the platform and the door was an enormous gap. I slipped and was about to fall headlong into it. Thankfully, Mum held me back by the half-belt.

That, essentially, is the whole story—nothing extraordinary. But this incident held such significance for Mum that she continued to recall it even on the eve of death. She'd smile and whisper just audibly—she'd lost her voice by then, and could only whisper:

"I'm pulling you by the half-belt and all I can think is, what if it snaps?"

Maidenhair, written in Zurich and Rome, also actually took its rise from Mum, or more precisely from her diary, which she gave me before her last operation. A thick oilskin notebook, its yellowed pages covered with pencil notes—written not, I may add, in the "clinical" hand I was used to, but in a cosier, more girlish one. Mum began it when she was in her final year of school and continued writing in it for several years as a student. This was the end of the forties and the very beginning of the fifties.

I remember her telling me about the persecution of the "cosmopolites" in her institute, during which its best professors disappeared. But there's no mention of that in the notebook. It's a most ordinary girl's diary: yearning for someone to love, she listens anxiously to her heart—has the feeling already come over her, is it the real thing? And it radiates a great deal of happiness. From books she'd read, from girlfriends, from the sun outside the window, from the rain. Its pages are awash with the unthinking youthful confidence that life will give you more than you asked of it.

It contains no traces of the fear that had gripped the country. As if there were no denunciations, no camps, no arrests, no queues, no penury.

I read it then and marvelled at the naivety of that blind girl who could not see what she had fallen into.

That girl was born into a prison nation, into darkness, yet she still looked upon her life as a gift, as an opportunity to realise herself in love, to give love, to share her happiness with the world.

When I found out that Mum's diary, too, had perished in the fire, I felt its continued grip on me. And at some point I realised: no, this was not the naivety and folly of a silly young girl who had failed to understand what was going on around her, this was the wisdom of the one who has sent, does send and always shall send girls into this world, no matter what hell we've turned it into.

The world around is cold and dark, but into it has been sent a girl so that, candle-like, she might illuminate the all-pervasive human darkness with her need for love.

Mum loved to sing, but knew she had no voice, and felt embarrassed. She'd sing when there was no one to hear her. Most often she sang what she used to listen to as a child. One of her favourite singers was Izabella Yurieva. My father had some old recordings of her romances, and would often put them on when we were still living together in the basement on Starokonyushenny Lane and in Presnia.

I was convinced then that all these voices from old records belonged to people long since dead. Stalin and Ivan the Terrible were much of a muchness to me—the distant past. Then it suddenly transpired that Izabella Yurieva was still alive, her records started being re-released and she began making television appearances. You could even go and see her at the House of Actors. I never did get to meet her while she was still alive.

When the singer died, I was staggered to learn that she'd lived a hundred years—she was born in 1899 and died in 2000—the entire monstrous, accursed Russian twentieth century.

I wanted to write about what I had felt and understood thanks to Mum's diary. I started writing about Bella. The result was *Maidenhair*.

Little of the singer's life remains—there are no diaries, no memoirs, leaving us with no more than a spare outline of her life story. In those years people were afraid of their own past—it was impossible to tell what might later put you in mortal danger. Danger might spring from any source: past meetings, things said, letters. People would destroy their past, would strive to rid themselves of it.

I wanted to restore her obliterated life to her. I began writing her reminiscences and diaries.

As far as possible, it was important for me not to fabricate anything. For example, I would pick out real-life accounts from the memoirs of people living in pre-revolutionary Rostov, restoring to my Bella her actual teachers at the Bilinskaya Gymnasium in Khakhladzhev House on Taganrog Prospect, the clerk in the Joseph Pokorny stationary shop on Sadovaya Street, where she bought her exercise books and quills, and that gymnasium porter who, having read "Kholstomer," bequeathed his skeleton to an anatomical cabinet.

Detail by detail, I restored her vanished life history to her.

She never did anything but sing—like that grasshopper from the fable. Only in real life the survival of the ants building that Babelian ant-hill up to the heavens and turning into camp dust depended no less on her singing than on supplies for the winter. She was the proverbial candle that illuminated, however faintly, their darkness. She sang to the slaves about love. She helped them preserve human dignity.

I was eager to restore her life to her, if only in a book—and there's no other way in any case.

Of course, much in the life of Izabella Yurieva wasn't the same as in my Bella's.

But I know that when she and I finally meet, Izabella Danilovna shall forgive me and say:

"Don't worry yourself! Everything's fine. Thank you kindly!"

And now I return to the rest home on the Volga, where the woods are full of wild strawberries and everyone is still alive.

I see images from that time:

The herringbone brick path leading to the canteen.

The defiled nearby forest, strewn with scraps of paper, bottles, greasy newspapers.

The Volga in a downpour, white with frothy foam, as if there's laundry being done.

We've been mushroom picking in the faraway forest and are taking the track homewards, but our eyes still can't stop searching, and rove about the track verges.

And now, having gone for a morning swim in the Volga, Mum and I are coming back to our little house. We walk barefoot over the wet moss, dew seeping up between our toes. We climb the porch steps, already warmed through by the sun, and Mum draws my attention to our rapidly disappearing tracks:

"See, I'm flatfooted!"

Our room on a hot day: mushroom dampness, the curtains are held together by a pin, the wallpaper's curling and bulging, and Mum closes the creaky cabinet door, sticking a piece of cardboard into the crack so it doesn't open.

And now I see the boozer in the nearest town—Uncle Vitya's popped in for just a moment, and there we stand, Mum and I, waiting a good half hour for him in the heat, and still he won't come out.

I kept waiting for Uncle Vitya to ask me about Dad, but he never did, right up until the very last moment.

The night before we left I woke up with the thought that someday Mum would die. I lay there in the darkness and listened to her puffing in her sleep, snoring herself awake, then, after much tossing and turning, puffing away once again. I remember this acute sense of pity which wouldn't let me get back to sleep. It was strange somehow—she lay there in the bed next to mine, very much alive, and at the same time it was like she'd already died. Also, I really needed the loo. The houses had no toilets. During the day you had to go to a rather unpleasant establishment that stank to high heaven of chlorine, but at night I'd just find a spot somewhere near the porch.

I got up quietly and went out, carefully closing the door behind me.

Damp, mist, cold night air. The cusp of daybreak.

I stopped at the nearest bush. Steam rose from the stream.

And suddenly something happened to me. As if I'd stepped from the unreal into the real. As if, like a lens twisted into focus, all my senses had been sharpened. As if the whole world around me had donned my skin, chilled in the August morning frost.

I looked around and couldn't understand what was going on: after all, I'd passed by this spot on so many occasions—and took notice of nothing; but now I saw, as if for the first time, that honeysuckle bush, and this rowanberry tree, and the towel forgotten on the washing line.

In the silence, sounds came forth from the mist: the distant hum of a motorboat on the river, the barking of dogs from the village on the far shore, the anxious call of a night bird, the whistle of a train at the station. Hoarse profanities floated in from the main road, accompanied by a girl's drunken guffaws.

And I heard myself breathing, heard my lungs gulping in life.

Suddenly I felt that I was no longer by a bush amidst the mist, but amidst the universe. No: I *was* the universe. That was the first time I experienced this remarkable sensation. And this was not only an anticipation of all my life to come. For the first time everything fused together, became a single whole. The smoke from an unseen bonfire and the wet rustling in the grass under my feet. Dad, who'd died no death, and Uncle Vitya, who'd asked no questions. What was and what would be.

Everything is still unnamed, nonverbal, because words for this do not exist.

And the Volga courses somewhere close by, swashing in the mist, but flows into no Caspian Sea.

And Mum died and yet lives still. She lies in her coffin with an Orthodox paper chaplet on her forehead, puffing away in her sleep in that rest home.

And everything melts into one: the half-belt overcoat, and Bobby Clarke's toothless grin, and Robert Walser's snowdrift, and that rickety 77 that never made it to Dorogomilovskaya Street, forcing us to splash our way through the puddles. And so, typing these words on my notebook, do I. As does the I now reading this line.

And the only way to die is to choke with happiness.

Translated by Leo Shtutin

Calligraphy Lesson

The capital letter, Sofia Pavlovna, is the beginning of all beginnings, so let us begin with that. It's like a first breath, a newborn's cry, you might say. Just a moment ago there was nothing. Absolutely nothing. A void. And for another hundred or thousand years there might still have been nothing, but suddenly this pen, submitting to an impossibly higher will, is tracing a capital letter, and now there's no stopping it. Being the pen's first movement toward the period as well, it is a sign of both the hope and the absurdity of what is. Simultaneously. The first letter, like an embryo, conceals all life to come, to the very end—its spirit, its rhythm, its force, and its image.

Don't go to any trouble, Evgeny Alexandrovich. I'm just a little chick and this is just my scratching. Why don't you tell me something amusing? Interesting things happen at your work every day, after all. All those crimes, murderers, prostitutes, and rapists.

Good God, what criminals? They're ordinary people. One blind drunk, another out of his mind, commit God knows what atrocity and are now thoroughly horrified themselves. We have no idea, they say, not a clue. And anyway, how could you even think that I, fine, upstanding man that I am, might do something like that? So they write petitions and solicitations and then more petitions and solicitations, begging for mercy, but no one has the slightest notion of how to hold a pen. Allow me to demonstrate.

Lay the left side of the middle finger, down by the nail, against the right side of the pen. Like this. Lay the thumb, also close to the nail, against the left side, and let the index finger rest but not press on top, as if it were stroking the pen's back. The pen rests against the base of the index finger's third joint. These three fingers are called the writing fingers. Neither the pinkie nor the ring finger should touch the paper. There should always be space, air, between the hand and the paper. If the hand is constrained and lies on the paper, if even the tip of the pinkie rests there, the wrist has no freedom of movement. The pen must touch the paper lightly, easily, without the least tension, as if it were simply playing. The pinkie and ring fingers, I assure you, are nothing but bestial atavisms, and one can both write and make the sign of the cross without them.

You see, I can never get anything right. For instance, a few days ago I decided to drown myself. Really, don't laugh. I dashed off a note and taped it to the mirror. But first, for some unknown reason, I decided to stop in at the bathhouse. I have no idea why. Oddly enough, I remember this one sturdy woman washing her red hair across from me. She was sprinkled all over with freckles—on her breasts, her belly, her back, her legs. Her hair was thick and long and soaked up so much water that when she straightened up, the washtub was nearly empty and an entire waterfall came crashing down into it. When I finally got to the bridge, a barge was drifting by below. The men down there shouted something and laughed, as if to say, Come on, jump! I waited for it to pass, but right behind came another barge and another. They kept shouting and laughing from each one and there was no end to those barges in sight. All of a sudden it struck me as funny, too, so I went home, arriving before anyone else, thank God. I took down the note, grabbed a loaf of bread, and gobbled up the whole thing practically. Actually, this is all totally beside the point. Go on. Now where were we?

Why don't we move on to the line then? But first, sit up straight and relax your shoulders. You can't write hunched over or at attention. You see, at the basis of everything is the line, the stroke. Take any two points in space, any two objects, and you can draw a line connecting them. There are these invisible strokes between all the things in the world. They make everything interconnected, unseverable. Distance is totally irrelevant. These lines can stretch like rubber bands, which only makes the connections between objects stronger. You see, there's a line stretching between the inkwell and this ace that fluttered down to the parquet, between the piano pedal and the branches' shadow on the windowsill, between you and me. It's like a tendon that keeps the world from falling apart. The pen-drawn line is that connection materialized, so to speak. And letters are nothing but strokes, or lines, held together by knots and loops for stability. The pen ties the line to the form, the shape, and endows it with meaning and spirit—humanizing it, so to speak. Try to draw a straight line! All right, now admire this trembling curly hair. Mortals can't draw a straight line. A straight line is nature's unattainable ideal toward which myriad curves aspire. Just as letters cling pell-mell, so too do they all have an inherent harmony and beauty—in the symmetry of their curves, the impetuosity of their slant, the correctness of their proportions. The pen is merely the registrar that faultlessly imprints on paper every dream and fear, every virtue and vice, taking us by the arm each time we press down. Everything that happens in your life immediately ends up on the tip of your pen. Tell me about someone, and I'll tell you exactly what kind of handwriting that person has.

So start on me.

You are magnificent. You are extraordinary. You have no idea how wonderful you are. And your handwriting, Tatiana Dmitrievna, is pure, fresh, childlike. The letters actually get bigger as they approach the end of the line.

You mustn't go on like that, Evgeny Alexandrovich! You're much too kind. Just look at a bit of my writing. Take this. No, better this. No, don't. Never mind about my handwriting. You're nothing but a sly widower, chasing after me, and now you're spinning tales for this gullible, simplehearted woman. I can see right through you even without any handwriting. After all, you aren't indifferent toward me, isn't that so? Well then, declare your love right now, this instant. Not that any of this matters. Better not to say anything.

Just think, it's been eight whole years since my Olya's been gone. I'm not saying she died, of course. I haven't told anyone about this since it happened, but I'll tell you. She and I had been through so much, but for better or worse we'd survived it all together, and suddenly I found myself living with a complete stranger, someone I didn't know at all. At one point Olya's right eye started to dim and she started going blind. I took her to Moscow, found a specialist, and they operated. Thank God, she recovered. After that, every six months, and later even more often, she went back for checkups. Whenever I asked, she would say everything was fine, but it felt like she was leaving something out. I was afraid Olya was going blind and wasn't telling me. She'd changed a lot. She was withdrawn, got annoyed over the least thing, and often cried at night. Before, she'd loved to read Kolya his little books in the evening; now she wouldn't touch them. I was frightened. I wanted to help somehow, realized there was nothing I could do, and loved her all the more because of it. And then one day at dinner Olya was pouring tea and the china teapot broke right in her hands. We got splashed and jumped up, at which point Olya started screaming that she couldn't go on like this, that she hated herself but she hated me even more, that she didn't go to Moscow to see any specialist but to see a man who loved her and whom she loved. I was having a hard time understanding what she was saying. "What do you want?" I asked. "I want to not see you!" Olya started screaming again. "I'd rather hang myself, but I'm not going to go on living like this. I'm leaving you for him. I love him." "And Kolya? What about Kolya?" She started to weep. "But this whole thing is impossible," I said. "I can't live without Kolya, nor Kolya without you. You want to abandon your son? Kolya can't go through his whole life being ashamed of his mother and despising her. That's not going to happen. It can't." "I know," I heard in reply, "you wish I were dead! Fine! I'll die!" She jumped up and ran out of the room. I tried to hold her back. "That's crazy! Stop it!" She broke away and locked herself in her room. I got scared and started pounding on the door, but Olya suddenly opened it and in an almost calm voice said, "You don't have to break the door down. Everything's fine." The next day at breakfast, in front of Kolya, she announced there was something wrong with her eyes again and she was going to the clinic in Moscow tomorrow. What could I say? Kolya and I went to see his mama off at the station. Olya was crying and kept kissing and hugging Kolya. The boy kept breaking away and asking her to bring him back a rifle. The next morning a telegram arrived from Ryazan. Olya had fallen ill en route. She'd been taken off the train and had died right there at the station. The telegram had arrived while I was out. When I ran in from work, everyone had gray, tear-stained faces, only they hadn't said anything to Kolya. The boy had been badgering everyone. "What happened? Is something wrong with Mamochka?" "Oh no," I told him. "Everything's fine, everything's fine." That same night I went to get her. I had to ride all night. My traveling companion complained of insomnia and suggested we play chess. We moved our men around until morning. From time to time I'd forget, but when I remembered what had happened and where I was going, I'd start wailing. My neighbor would shudder and give me a frightened look. The train car shook, the chessboard shuddered, and the men kept slipping off their squares. Then I would stop wailing and right them. Olya—a beautiful stranger wearing a dress I'd never seen—met me at the station early in the morning. When she saw me she waved and burst into sobs. My first impulse was to slap her across the face. I could barely restrain myself. "What's going on?" She only shook her head, unable to utter a word. Her whole body was quaking. I sat her down on a bench. "Listen, Kolya doesn't know anything. Let's go home and explain that it was a misunderstanding!" At last Olya got a hold of herself. "Don't interrupt me," she said. "I've made my decision no matter what you all think of me. The space in the baggage car is paid for. There are some minor details left: the lining and the ribbons. The train is at seven this evening. We'll make it." It was all crazy and impossible, and I followed her around in a daze. At the store she took a long time and kept finding fault with the fabric and ribbons. Nothing pleased her. Either the colour didn't go or the material was crummy. She dragged me to another store, and then we went back to the first. We went to one office and then another and another. By six a coffin lined in blue ruches and bows was in a separate room at the station. She'd even thought of that. We stopped in at the refreshment stand. She looked starkly at her plate and swallowed in silence. I couldn't help it; I started shouting. "But what about Kolya?" "I'm going to have another child," she said calmly. I recoiled for fear I might kill her. On the way back, to avoid questions, I rode in the mail car. The sleepy worker sorting the mail mumbled, "I've shipped lots of these dead folks in my life. Like some tea?" I declined. He slurped away at it for a long time, then lay down and started to snore. The car rocked, and everything rumbled and shook. In the light from the night lamps you could see the cockroaches crawling in from everywhere. Next to me, behind a wooden partition, was the empty coffin. I was in shock. I couldn't imagine that morning would come and there would be a funeral. The whole time, I kept seeing Kolya asking his mama to bring him back a rifle. It felt like the end of the world, like there would be no coming day or life thereafter. There couldn't. But then morning came and a hearse met me at the station. There were many tears, laments, and sighs and even more fuss and commotion. They wanted to take the coffin back to the house, but I insisted it be sent directly to the church. I instructed that under no circumstance should the lid be opened. Seeing Kolya was what scared me the most. When I entered his room, he threw himself into my arms. He sobbed and I walked him around the room, kissing his soft, dear, sweet-smelling nape. "Our Mamochka is gone forever now," I whispered. The funeral was the next day. People shook my hand and said things. Many were just pretending to be sorry, I could tell, and out of the corner of my ear I heard something bad said about Olya. Her mother arrived, a woman trying to look younger than her age, wearing perfume and dressed in black, but elegantly. I thought with horror that she too might be party to this cruel joke, but when she saw the coffin, she started crying and demanding it be opened. "Show me my little girl! I don't care what happened to her. I want to see her one last time!" I barely managed to talk her out of it. At the funeral banquet everyone kept trying to get me to drink. "Drink up, Evgeny Alexandrovich! Believe me, you'll feel better!" But I didn't so much as touch my glass. The evening after the funeral, I could barely get Kolya to bed, he was crying so. I was going to read him a little something, but he suddenly looked at me with angry, hate-filled eyes. "Stop it, Papa. How could you!" I went on leave and took Kolya to Yalta to let the child regain his senses and clear his head. At first the boy seemed to be walking in his sleep, oblivious to everything and refusing to eat. Then a woman moved into the dacha next door with her three sons, who were a little older than Kolya, and the company of boys quickly distracted him.

They raced around from morning to night, flew into rages, and fought. Imperceptibly, Kolya grew tanner, taller, and stronger and got to be a good swimmer. One time at the beach, when he and I were there together, he suddenly dove under and for the longest time did not appear above the water. I jumped to my feet, started running, and was about to dive in myself when he popped up in a completely different spot and started beating the water with his fists: "Scared ya!" he shrieked joyously through the splashing. "Scared ya!" Kolya ran around barefoot all the time so his feet toughened up and every evening I greased his hardened, callused heels, to keep them from cracking. At first, that woman from Syzryan came on strong with stories about her creep of a husband, but before long she backed off and started hanging around with some well-built Greek. A year later I received a letter from Olya, from Kiev for some reason. The handwriting was uneven, but it was hers, even though the signature said Sorokina. Olya wrote that she'd given birth to a marvelous little girl, she and her husband adored each other, and she couldn't be happier.

But quite a few years have passed and you're still alone, Evgeny Alexandrovich.

How can I explain it, Nastasya Filippovna? One day I had to stay late at work. I was writing up a report. I think it was about some young man who'd killed the mother of his buddy, who was in the army at the time. They tracked the youth down the same day, and he didn't deny it but kept insisting she'd gotten him drunk and lured him on. A photograph was attached to the case materials—a naked body on the floor, fat and misshapen. There are pictures like that in nearly every file. It's nothing unusual. By the time I left, it was dark outside, a cold autumn evening, and I started home. Where else could I go? When Kolya still lived at home, I'd always tried to get back as early as I could to feed him, check his homework, play a game. We would cut out little paper men, draw faces on them, and invent all kinds of stories. Kolya had an amazing imagination. He would come up with great yarns and he was always rescuing everyone. Kolya would talk about himself nonstop: about the other kids, his teachers, his grades, all his friendships and arguments. But now I had to force myself to go home to an empty house. So that day, knowing I faced another endless, pointless evening, I took the longest possible route home, then made another detour, and walked like that for an hour, maybe two—aimlessly, I thought—and suddenly found myself outside your house. There was no one outside and the streetlights were dark. I opened the gate and walked in. It was dark in the garden. The only light came from the windows. I got very close. The undrawn curtain revealed nearly half the room. No one was there. Suddenly you walked in and looked out the window, straight at me. That scared me and made me want to hide behind a tree, but I froze, transfixed. You were standing so close you couldn't have not seen me, but you didn't even flinch. You turned to one side, then the other, ran your palms over your hips, looking at your reflection, fixed your hair, turned away, and walked through the room and around the table. You were talking to yourself. I couldn't hear through the double window. I could just see your lips moving. Suddenly your husband loomed up. He'd been lying on the sofa the whole time, and now he stood up, in his robe, disheveled, with mussed hair and a tired, sleepy face. He must have taken a nap right after work. He put his arms around you, lay his head on your shoulder, and shut his eyes. Then the children were brought in, to say goodnight probably, because they were wearing their nightshirts and were all pink under the lampshade. You made a cross over your daughter and son and kissed them on the forehead. The little girl kept holding out a book to you, probably trying to talk you into reading to her before bed. First you shook your head and your face was stern, but your little girl begged you so, so you smiled and sat down next to her in the armchair. Your child wiggled for a long time getting comfortable and then fell still with her little mouth open, on a flight of fancy to a land of trolls, or naughty ducks, or enchanted frogs, places you and I can never be. Meanwhile your spouse started a game of blind man's buff with your son, put a coin in his eye to look like a monocle, and paddling with his arms, chased the little boy around the room. The child was in such ecstasy that his cries, shrieks, and laughter splashed out the window and scattered over the stiff, chilly garden. You tried to calm them both down a few times and spoke sternly, probably about how the children shouldn't get so worked up before bedtime, or words to that effect, but even you couldn't help laughing and gave first one and then the other a playful smack with your little book. The coin popped out and your husband got down on his hands and knees to reach under the chair for it, whereupon the boy jumped on his neck and the girl on her papa's back. You were all laughing hard. Finally, the children were taken off to bed. Your spouse lit up and sat down with the newspaper under a lamp in a corner of the sofa. You settled in beside him with a fat book. Then you got up, brought a pillow over, plumped it up at the other end of the sofa, and lay down, wrapping your legs in a big warm throw. You read like that for a long time, with your legs draped across his knees. Once you looked into the corner together—up. It was the clock chiming. Occasionally he would read you something out loud, some funny item. He would laugh and shake his head while he read, but you would just smile faintly, not even looking up, you were so engrossed in your book. Then he folded the paper, yawned, said something to you, you just nodded, and he went out. You kept reading, first sitting with your legs curled underneath you, then lying on your back. From time to time you would take a pin out of your hair and scratch your head. I didn't notice how cold it was, that I was chilled through, but I just couldn't leave. I kept standing there watching you. At one point you stood up and took a box of candy from the sideboard, balanced it on your knees, and ate piece after piece, wadding each wrapper up in a ball and flicking it away. Suddenly, from upstairs, came a child's cry. You jumped up, dropped your book on the table, and rushed out of the room looking frightened. No one was there for a long time. Then your husband appeared for a moment and the light went out. But I kept standing there. I was afraid to leave.

Oh, you naughty boy! Have you no shame? Gray hair, and you behave like a little boy. It's true, my husband is always reading things out loud from the newspapers. For instance, recently there was one story about three men convicted of raping a girl, a teenager. Not only that, but imagine, they were all reputable men and had families and children. In short, you never would have thought something like that about them. Understandably, they were angry and indignant, and they hired the best lawyers. They brought charges against someone, saying it was all a frame-up. The girl was the daughter of their mutual acquaintances, though, and her parents believed everything she said and were furious at the base and vile things their good friends had done. During the inquiry and trial the girl told stories of such degenerate acts committed against her that no one ever doubted the veracity of her testimony. Such horrors simply could not have entered a child's mind. In short, they were convicted, but their lawyers kept active, another inquiry was scheduled, and the upshot was that the three were innocent, that the girl was sick, that she had an erotically based psychological deviance and had dreamed this all up and believed her own fantasies. The convicted men were released, of course. One can only imagine the joy in their unfortunate families. And they placed the girl in a special clinic to teach this horrible girl not to defame honest people. After all was said and done, though, they found details in her initial statements that simply could not have been invented: an unusual birthmark in a most intimate place and something else like that. Other testimony and evidence were found as well. Finally, one of them confessed and all three were imprisoned again, this time for good. But meanwhile, what was most interesting was they didn't release the girl, because she really was abnormal and attacked everyone, men and women alike. In short, a fine lot all. But you just don't know my husband really. He's a marvelous man and I love him very much. This is a man worthy of every respect. He loves me and our children very much. He's always coming up with surprises, For instance, he writes either me or himself letters and mails them, and then we open them together and he watches me—after all, he only does it to bring me pleasure—and I go into ecstasies over his silly scribbles, to make him feel good. I rushed headlong into marriage. This very young fool fell head over heels in love with a grown man just because he visited our house occasionally and never said a word. Now I realize my primitive curiosity fed my fantasy—so that I couldn't go on living without this clam. Later, after the wedding, I had an epiphany. It was like I'd regained my senses. I was horrified at what I'd done, but our son showed up so I resigned myself. This man is a marvelous husband, and I understand intellectually that I should be grateful to him, but it's unbearable. The strange, crazy ways he has of eating disgust me. He always has his second course first and then his soup. He likes to crumble bread into his milk because his mama made him a mush like that when he was little, and he shovels that mess, that awful, swelling swill, into both cheeks. I'm always finding his socks in the most incredible places, and when he loses something, it's my fault. He can go weeks without a bath and his dirty hair smells awful, but before leaving for work he spends fifteen minutes putting on cologne, to mask the smell. When he thrusts himself on me, especially at night, I try to imagine it's someone else instead of him. Don't get the wrong idea. I have no thought of cheating on him; I would despise myself afterward. If I fell in love with someone else, I would fight the feeling in any case. Self-respect is more important than pleasure. I have children and a home and I can't imagine a different life for myself, although in my mind I'm cheating on him constantly—disgusting, horrible, filthy thoughts, and I try to drive them out, but I can't. And that's even worse than cheating on him for real. Sometimes I scare myself. And that goes not just for my husband but for the thoughts that overwhelm me in general. It's become impossible. When I was nursing our first child, I was so tired, I was in a state of such nervous agitation over his endless illnesses and my chronic lack of sleep, I was so tormented by his screaming and crying, that one day I had a nervous breakdown, a moment of insanity. In the middle of the night the boy started screaming again and I jumped up, exhausted, and suddenly such hatred bubbled up inside me, such rage, such fury, that I was ready to kill him. I actually snatched the child from his crib—I remember I was suddenly struck by the idea of throwing him off the balcony. This horrified me so that things suddenly felt crazyafter all, I was a second away from the irrevocable. After that night, my milk dried up. Listen to me, because it would never occur to a mother to kill her own child!

What are you talking about! At work I deal with stories you could never even imagine, but you know I've gotten used to it and I do my job. One man, for instance, quarreled with his wife and slaughtered her and their two children with the bread knife. The older was four and the younger was an infant. Then he came to his senses and started to slit his own veins, and while he was bleeding, he set fire to the apartment and jumped out the window. Another forced his daughter to sleep with him, and that very night she killed him with an ax. A third beat his brother to death with a log because they couldn't figure out how to divide up the house they'd inherited. A fourth tortured twins, neighbor children, raped them, poked out their eyes, and left them to die in an abandoned cellar—and then went through the worry with their parents, acted outraged, and took part in the searches, until they happened to expose him. You wake up, have breakfast, get ready for work, and you already know what's going to happen. One man choked his own mother with a stocking and carried the body to the outhouse piece by piece, and I said to him: "Please sign here!" And so it goes, day after day, year after year. If it's not Peter, it's Nikolai; if it's not the doting father, it's the loving son. Tomorrow, the day after tomorrow, a hundred years from now. The words, even those are the same: I didn't see it. I wasn't there. It wasn't me. Nor is the charge ever very original: "consumed by an unquenchable thirst for gain," "blinded by envy, tormented by his awareness of being a nobody," "the scum, having lost all humanity, to satisfy a moment's fancy," "after foully taking advantage of the helplessness of his father, who was crippled by paralysis," "who for twenty years cleverly and perfidiously concealed his criminal essence under a mask of decency." And the defense babbles on the same way: "made desperate by the hopelessness and pointlessness of his pitiful existence;" "having no other way to defend his profaned honor;" "being a victim of a prison education—since if you're born in prison all you've seen around you since childhood is rapists and murderers;" "Yes, blood was spilled, and the instrument of murder is before you, but look at the remorse this unfortunate man has shown! Instead of convicting him, share the grief of a man who murdered his own son!" ; "My God, even you must have been thoroughly oiled and felt a wild, half-bestial, half-childish desire to take revenge on someone for your good-for-nothing, betrayed life, for all the agonies and injustices, for everything you've suffered at the hands of people near and far, God, and your own self. Haven't you?" They do things even they can't imagine, and I tell them, Write, now, to keep from losing your mind, write a final word not in some lapidary cursive but, say, an elegant, bubbly Rondo, in blurred letters that repeat, but the verdict is in a littera fractura with flourishes, or Gothic logjams, or Batard, or Coulé, or whatever strikes your fancy, one page like this, another like that. Even if you only write one word, to say nothing of a page, make it harmony itself, so that its regularity and beauty offset that whole crazy world, that whole caveman mindset. Why just today they convicted someone who had poisoned her husband, a drunkard and a brawler, someone the long-suffering household members may have needed to be freed from long ago because their children are cretins, monsters. She tried to hang herself in her cell, but they cut her down and at the hearing she said, "Do whatever you want. You're nobody to me because I'm still going to kill myself. I'm not going to live, and the Highest Court will vindicate me, because I'm fed up with living." That's what she said. But our presiding judge said, "But you see, dear, that's us. We are the Highest Court, and whether you are or aren't fed up is not for you to decide!" But she kept up her muttering: "I'm fed up with this life of yours." That's what I wrote: fed up. Невтерпёж! What that one word costs! Just try it! The primitive *H* may not merit special mention. Its crossbar is written on a slant in a single stroke. You place the tip of your pen at the beginning, then bend your fingers right away, and the pen itself pulls you down, but the main thing here is the pressure. God forbid you press too hard or lift too much because the line isn't supposed to breathe! The flamelike shape—because it does resemble a tongue of flame—bends first to the left, then the right. It gets fatter in the middle and dwindles to nil at the ends. On the third beat the stick has a curve at the bottom. The first five sections of the line are drawn straight, but on the sixth the pressure eases up and the line, rounding, drifts off to the right, ending at the invisible line that confines each letter to its allotted space, its cell, you might say. Below, where the stick curves, between the imagined field of the cell and the tip of the line it contains, you get an empty corner. After the curve the fine line goes up—not straight up but in an arc—bending slightly to the right so as not to lose contact with the page and break through to the *ё*, a cunning ninny, unprepossessing to look at, but demanding caution and deft treatment in order to achieve the desired end. After the clumsy, snub-nosed *Н*, the *е* requires a light, graceful line that begins with an eyelash stroke and a bend to the right, cuts across the middle evenly on an incline, flies back after the bend, nearly grazing the ceiling of its chamber, and as it falls back in its noose rushes into the half-oval with pressure on the left side; moreover the bend of the capillary outline is hidden in the half-oval but is not left behind. After a break the pen heads all the way to the upper corner of the next cell. The merest tremble or thickening could instantly destroy the illusion of this free soaring, which takes a drastic gain in altitude to become a *в*. The secret essence of this spindleleg lies by no means in the spaces that run through it from top to bottom but in the concluding, unremarkable, but danger-laden sign-off loop beyond which the *т* is already twitching impatiently. Here it's important not to be too hasty in imprinting the tightening loop but to wait for the loop to turn almost into a period. Then you can rush headlong into three holes in a row, returning happily once again to the *е*, *р*, and *п*, which is hardly a letter, just a *г* on a stick. But onward, onward, to the very end and the *ж*, that amazing, anthropod peahen, the only one that falls into a full five beats! There's something of the two-headed eagle to it and at the same time its soft half-ovals sit firmly on the line, like on a perch. It seems to clamp an unraveling world together—heaven and earth, east and west. It's elegant, perfect, and sufficient unto itself. And now, if the hand was true, if the pen didn't shake once, if everything came together, then, you won't believe it, a miracle takes place at my desk! A sheet of ordinary paper breaks free and rises above events! Its perfection immediately yields an alienation, a hostility even, toward all that exists, toward nature itself, as if another, higher world, a world of harmony, had wrested this space from that kingdom of worms! They may hate and kill each other, betray and hang themselves there, but it's all just raw material for my penmanship, fodder for beauty. And during those astounding minutes, when you feel like writing nonstop, you experience a strange, inexpressible feeling. Truly, this is happiness!

Evgeny Alexandrovich, you're insane!

You don't understand, Anna Arkadievna. Going mad is the privilege of God's fools, a reward for the elect, but we are all being punished for something. The main thing is that there's no one to ask what for. Judge for yourself. Take my Kolya. When he went to Moscow to study, I was happy for him, my son, who had suddenly, imperceptibly, turned into a young man, a university student with a sparse, impatient little beard. Less than two months later I received a document, a notification, saying my son was under investigation, charged with murder. I dropped everything and rushed to Moscow. The investigator in charge of the case told me that my Kolya and his friend had attacked and killed some young woman. Kolya was caught, but the second youth slipped away. "Are you in your right mind?" I shouted. "Yes. The scoundrel has confessed to everything." I didn't believe a word of it. I knew there had been some mistake, some horrible misunderstanding. Finally they allowed us a visit. Kolya hadn't changed at all. He was even wearing the same jacket. He'd just let his beard grow out. "Kolya, why did you confess?" I began. "After all, it wasn't you!" I thought he would throw his arms around me, cry, and tell me everything that had happened, but he started talking about which petitions I needed to write and to whom, asked me to remember everything exactly and not get mixed up, and got angry when I couldn't seem to. That's what he said to me: "Father, wake up and remember this!" And he was beside himself that I hadn't brought any money. All I had with me were a few small bills. "Papa," he said, "if you have money, you can live anywhere, even in prison." And still I didn't believe the investigator or Kolya. I still don't. My boy could not have done that. He slandered himself. Out of fear. Someone had put the fear of God in him. But Kolya might have been trying to protect or save someone, too. At trial he was so nervous, he tried so hard to fight his fear, that instead he was brash, slouched in his chair, and answered questions with a smirk. When the witness, a janitor, got his testimony mixed up, Kolya actually started laughing. And he shrugged at his terrible sentence—fifteen years—as if to say, Imagine. He's just a little boy, a silly little boy, a child. As they were leading him away, he shouted, "Papa, don't cry. I love you!" The parents of the murdered girl were sitting right there in the courtroom. During the hearing the mother would start sobbing from time to time, and then the father would take her out of the room, but after a while they would return and take their seats again. The first day of the trial I went over to them and wanted to say something, I didn't know what—beg their forgiveness, plead for mercy—but they wouldn't let me say a word. "Get away!" the father shouted. I collected Kolya's things, wrote endless, pointless requests and petitions, and sat in reception rooms for hours just to clarify where they were sending him. I'd already made plans to visit him in the summer. Maybe they'd let me if I asked my boss for a special meeting. But that summer I got sick and took to my bed, and I never did take my trip to the distant and terrible Ivdel. Kolya's letters were brief: what to send in the package, where to write the next pointless mercy letter, as he put it. A year passed that way. At work they didn't know anything about Kolya, or maybe they were pretending they didn't, because before that they would occasionally ask, "How's that son of yours?" and now it was all about cases, as if I'd never had Kolya. And then one day I was asked to stop in to see our Viktor Valentinovich. I went into his office and stood there, waiting, but he was clearly uneasy and started pacing around the room, asked me to have a seat, and for a long time didn't say anything. Then he mumbled, "Really, I don't even know how to begin this conversation. You see, the problem is that your son—" I interrupted him. "Yes, my Kolya was convicted, but he's not guilty of anything, it's a mistake, he slandered himself!" "Please, wait!" he put a document in front of me. "Your son has escaped." For a long time after that I couldn't think clearly. Viktor Valentinovich brought me some water, put his hand on my shoulder, and said, "Get a grip," and something else. Then he started saying Kolya would quite likely come home sooner or later, but regardless, he was a dangerous criminal and I as a decent man whose honesty no one doubted would let them know as soon as he showed up. "Yes yes, of course." It felt like I was dreaming. I nodded and went to continue my writing. A long time has passed since that day, but still no Kolya. Sometimes I look out the window in the evening and it feels like he's somewhere nearby, in the darkness, behind the trees. He's hiding, afraid to come out. I open a small window and call out softly, so only he can hear, "Kolya! Kolya!"

Pay no attention to me, Evgeny Alexandrovich, I just remembered something that happened yesterday. You don't know whether to laugh or cry. You know Zhdanov? Well, you've seen him at our house—a second cousin twice removed and a dreadful self-centered fool. I happened to be home alone. My husband had gone on an inspection tour, little Sasha was with his grandmother, and Vova's been in college for two months. Out of the blue, Zhdanov showed up. "Larochka," he said with a leer, "I came to have my way with you!" "What's this, Zhdanov? Has passion got the better of you? You know I never thought of myself as a femme fatale!" "Passion? Hardly. It's just that you talk so much about morality that this will be my last argument in our debate. I came merely to tempt you and lead you into sin, that's all." "But you're repulsive, Zhdanov!" I told him. "Believe me, that doesn't matter!" and he reached under my skirt. I wanted to laugh, slap him, pour water over his bald head, but I was overtaken by apathy, passivity. I can't explain. It all just happened, moreover I felt nothing, absolutely nothing. Zhdanov grunted and wheezed and growled. Then he stretched out across the bed, flopping his belly to one side, and lit up. I said, "What a smart aleck you are, Mishenka! I just might go and fall in love with you!" And he said, "What do you mean? I love my wife and children." He finished smoking and reached for me again. Suddenly there was a noise in the front hall. Before I could figure out who it might be, my husband was standing in the doorway. Dead silence. Finally Zhdanov said, "Well, time for me to go!" and started pulling on a sock. My husband hemmed and hawed in a strange, old womanish voice. "Didn't you see the telegram? I left it by the mirror. Vova's coming home today. They gave him leave." "And here he comes!" Zhdanov said, pointing out the window. Indeed, Vova was opening the gate, wearing his uniform—smart, grown-up, handsome. We rushed to get dressed. Zhdanov couldn't seem to find his other sock, so he put his boot on his bare foot. My husband made the bed. I didn't even have time to put my dress on properly, let alone comb my hair! Vova fell on my neck immediately and then started hugging his father and then hugged Zhdanov. "Uncle Misha! Lord, how glad I am you're here! I love you all so much!" He grabbed a plate of pirozhki and started cramming them into his mouth, one after another, poor kid. I broke down in tears, kept kissing his prickly nape, his coarsened hands, his pimply cheeks, his sweat-soaked tunic. Zhdanov wanted to leave, but Vova wouldn't let him.

"Oh no, Uncle Misha, you're staying for dinner!" Vova told stories non-stop about the barracks, his idiot commanders, how you have to eat everything with a spoon and you practically have to fight to get an apple for dessert. The three of us behaved as if nothing special had just happened. And maybe nothing so terrible had. Before Vova could finish his cup he jumped up from the table, plopped down on the sofa, shut his eyes, and sighed. "God, this is great!"

Yes, you're quite right. Nothing so terrible! There was a silly embezzlement case that crossed my desk. This cashier, you see, a respectable type, a decent-looking man, had embezzled a lot of money. He denied all the charges and said he'd been put up to it by his thief of a boss. All in all he behaved like any honest man insulted by suspicions would. The whole case was proceeding toward acquittal. The defense presented spotless references and letters of praise for his many years of honest service. The man also won people's sympathy because his wife and three identically dressed sons were sitting in the courtroom in the front row. From time to time the father would buck them up, say something loudly across the entire courtroom—that they shouldn't cry, that he would certainly be acquitted because there was justice in this world, it could not fail. In essence, the entire case boiled down to a single note of a few lines submitted by the investigation. It had allegedly been written by the defendant and was proof of his guilt. Burinsky himself, the famous expert, was called in specially from Moscow to testify. Everything hinged on his opinion. So on the third day, I think, the case got to the point of his expert testimony. Burinsky rose—a large, stern, majestic man two heads taller than everyone else. Robinson himself would have envied that head of hair and beard. Everyone held their breath, gazing at the celebrity. He paused and then growled resoundingly, "This is the note." Burinsky shook the sheet of paper over his head. "And this is a handwriting sample." He shook another sheet. "And here is my conclusion. This man is innocent!" Pandemonium! The courtroom burst into applause and people were practically hugging each other. Burinsky sat back down and began raking his beard with an indifferent look on his face. A few formalities remained. The note, the letter, the handwriting taken for a sample, and the expert analysis lay on my secretarial desk. I couldn't believe my eyes. Both were written by the same person. "Wait a minute!" I exclaimed. "What do you mean? This is the same hand!" I felt the eyes of the entire courtroom on me. "Just look. Here and here!" Burinsky tossed back his gray curls and asked in amazement. "What are you actually implying?" "Look here. Can't you see?" I began explaining. "Just take the sweep of the pen. In handwriting the most important thing, after all, is the connection between letters. You can't forge or alter that. Just look at the *m*, *n*, and *н*. They're all drawn with their bottoms downward, like the *u*. And believe me, this is a sure graphological sign of goodness, openness, and emotional gentleness. These letters, on the contrary, were written with arches and betray secrecy and mendacity. Notice," I continued, "both in the note and in the letter, the pressure is not firm. No sooner does the pen touch the page than it encounters the paper's resistance, and an inevitable struggle ensues. A pen pressed into the paper reflects urge, will, obstinacy, contrariness, and belligerence. Here, rather, the hand is yielding, a sure sign of susceptibility, impressionability, sensitivity, delicacy, and tact. In both the letters are small, which indicates a sense of duty, self-restraint, and love for hearth and home. Note also how fat the letters are and how open they are at the top of the vowels. Altogether this is proof of credulity, peaceableness, a highly developed capacity for sympathy and deep attachment. Moreover, I dare say that this person possesses both taste and a sense of beauty. Just look at the elegant but perfectly unadorned capitals, at the wide, almost verselike left margin, at the indent, which starts nearly halfway across the page. The letters are almost not connected to each other, indicating a contemplative, lofty nature, detachment from the mundane, and a rich mental life. A signature without any flourishes indicates intellect. Oh, you have before you an exceptional person. Just look at the incredibly unique shape of the letters. Do they not, all else aside, betray a single patrimony for the neat letter and the messy note? The purely outward, superficial dissimilarity can be explained simply: the note was written in the dark, hence the interlacing of the uneven lines and the blind muddle of suddenly looming letters and words. You see, even a moment's inspection of these letters is enough to be convinced of their kinship. You have before you brothers and sisters in ink, twins from a single pen! This hook over the *й* alone is priceless, taking a running start and sliding into the question mark! And how could you ever confuse the adjacent *к* pinned to it? Or this *б*, which keeps trying to latch onto its neighbor? And the *ц*-you must take a close look at this little Jewess which Cyril abducted from Solomon's alphabet—all the grace in the steep line of her flaunted hip!" Everyone was silent, dumbstruck, but I kept talking and talking, powerless to stop myself. "Without a doubt, the person who wrote this is extraordinary, or rather, artistic. Hence the unevenness, the anxiety, the total lack of rhythm (which indicates emotional contentment), death poured outward for the time being. A tremendous, unconscious life force drives the ends of the line sharply upward. The diacriticals and the marks between the lines stretch and break off. They try to tear the word to shreds, annoyed over what has been left undone, unrealized, overlooked!" At this Burinsky rose from his seat. He walked toward the door, donning his hat as he went, and when he pulled even with me hissed through his teeth, "Fool!" Regardless, the court scheduled a second expert opinion, and of course they declared that the cashier had written the note. He was convicted, and after the hearing, while everyone was retrieving their coats in the checkroom, the judge came up to me and said, "God will punish you. Wait and see!" But it's all right. I'm alive. Alive, breathing, eating, and using up a stack of paper every day. My pen still scratches, punishes, and pardons. What's so important about that? I'm perfectly willing to admit that right now, this very minute, he may be whimpering from hunger, or freezing, or has had his teeth knocked out and is being raped by his cellmates, or that he's not even alive but lying in some morgue with a toe tag, or has simply faded away with time, written in cheap ink. Not that there's anything so awful about that. My God, what makes him any better than me or even you, that we should have regrets? Because there has yet to be a case, even the longest and most convoluted, at the end of which, when all was said and done, a pen did not place a period.

TRANSLATOR'S NOTE:

Like much of Mikhail Shishkin's writing, "Calligraphy Lesson" is highly allusive and attentive to the formal qualities of a story both inventively told and steeped in Russian atmospherics.

The reader will want to be aware of two issues in particular.

First, what the English reader may not realize—but the Russian will pick up instantly—is that the various women's names refer to characters from Russian classics: Sofia Pavlovna from Griboedov's play Woe from Wit; *Tatiana Dmitrievna from Pushkin's long poem* Evgeny Onegin; *Nastasia Filippovna from Dostoevsky's* Idiot; *Anna Arkadievna from Tolstoy's* Anna Karenina; *and Larochka (Lara) from Pasternak's* Doctor Zhivago.

Second, the passage describing the calligraphy of a specific Russian word—Невтерпёж—posed what was for me an unprecedented dilemma arising from the fact that in it Shishkin describes each letter as an object, yet the word's lexical meaning remains important.

The Russian word is colloquial, inappropriate for a court of law. Uttered by the defendant, this authentically felt word adds conviction and force to her statement. When the judge repeats it, he reinforces its power, but it's almost as if he's put quotes around it, so far is it from a judge's usual level of discourse. The narrator embeds the intense emotion the word has acquired in this context into his painstaking description of how each letter is to be written, but for him the act of writing is simultaneously a kind of self-protection. By focusing on the physical act of writing he is able to distance himself from the extreme human misery he witnesses over and over.

How could I convey the section's brilliant emotion but also truly translate it for the English reader? Should I or shouldn't I rewrite the passage to reflect the English cursive of the word's translation? It's a legitimate choice: the French translator decided to recast the passage to describe the word's French translation;

I decided to do both. I translated and reproduced the Russian word. In the pre-digital era, when Cyrillic characters were technically difficult to reproduce and so were rarely included in translations, I might have been inclined (or forced) to go the other way. Thanks to modern technology and to the fact that Shishkin's description was based on the letters' visual characteristics, which English readers could see and appreciate for themselves, I did not have to forgo Shishkin's tour de force (although I could not recreate his double-entendre: "г on a stick" is a euphemism for the Russian expression "shit on a stick," that is, something or someone utterly repulsive, worthless, or despicable).

Translating Shishkin means maintaining his virtuosic tension between complex detail and deeply felt emotion.

Marian Schwartz

The Blind Musician

How odd it felt to ring this doorbell while holding the cherished key tight in my pocket. To see again on the coatrack in the entryway her tasteless coat with the mother of pearl buttons. To walk through the rooms with all their brazen mirrors acting all innocent. To inhale the medicine smell that had once been completely aired out. To make as if I didn't know where the cotton balls were kept. To bear her stranger's hands holding the same lidded Chinese mug I'd fed him tea in like a little boy.

Zhenya,[6] my sweet Zhenya, I really think I'm better. I don't get dizzy anymore. I slept last night. True, I had an awful dream: I'd grown a beard. I rushed to the dream book and read that if the beard is long, that means honor and respect; if short, a trial. Lord, what drivel! Wait a little. Alexei Pavlovich will be home from work soon.

No no, Verochka Lvovna,[7] I'll just help you tidy up and be on my way.

But Zhenya, this might just be the healing action of the little gray housedress. Who knows? And the whole point was to get away from the hospital gown. Listen, there's no way I can thank you for all you've done for us. I do realize how unpleasant it is—the trips to the hospital, the bandages, the pus, the bedpan.

6 "Zhenya" is the diminutive of "Evgenia."

7 "Verochka" is the diminutive of "Vera."

Stop it! And don't you dare say those things ever again. Did they bring your prosthesis?

What prosthesis? It's an ordinary brassiere they've stuffed with something. Help me hook it up.

There, Verochka Lvovna, look how nice.

At home, in the dark entryway, I bumped into suitcases.

Zhenya, how you've grown! I barely recognize you! I remember you when you were this high! You and your father were always playing Gulliver. He'd spread his legs and shout, "Gulliver!" And you'd run back and forth, bubbling over with giggles. Remember? I came to visit and everyone here was hysterical because you'd eaten two apricots and swallowed the pits. The pits were sharp and got stuck in your bottom. Poor thing, you were wailing and no one knew what to do. They were just about to take you to the hospital, but I said, "Stop!" I washed my hands, poured oil over my finger, and in I went! I rotated one pit and both popped out as if they'd been shot from a cannon. And this is my Roman. Do you recognize my Roman? You were little when he and I came to visit and you played together. There was no leaving you alone for a minute or there'd be a fight. Remember how you ate all the candies and said it was him? I locked myself up in the bathroom with little Roman and took a belt to him. Immediately you pounded on the door: "Aunt Mika,[8] Aunt Mika, don't beat him, don't beat him, it was me!" You look so much like your papa, not at all like your mama. Your mama and I were like sisters. Here, look, this is us at the seashore, hugging, wearing identical swimsuits. That's what we told everyone, that we were sisters. Then she got married, became a provincial, and had you. That's where everything happened to

8 "Mika" is the diminutive of "Mirra."

your mama, too. We aren't staying long, Zhenya dear. Your papa wrote, "Stay as long as you like." But we're here just a little while. Once Roman passes his exams, we'll find an apartment. How pretty you've become! May Roman touch your face?

Kind Alexei Pavlovich, something's happened. Oh no, as always the ardor of my feelings raises no doubts. But in the last few days, I admit, I haven't been able to shake a sensation that I can't bring myself to put into words. Just like in *Gulliver,* the picture, remember? You're the cook, you're plucking a turkey, I'm sewing something, and suddenly a face peeks in the window, only it's not a face of our—Lilliputian—proportions. The turkey falls to the floor. The needle jabs my finger, and the people we'd imagined ourselves to be up to that moment, whose lives were special and happy, are thrown into disarray. But I knew you were right before, you know. It only seems that you're sculpting me in your own image and likeness, whereas in this reality, rainy since morning, you yourself are merely the fruit of my fantasies, a perfectly commonplace occurrence in *belles lettres*. Apparently, it doesn't take a great mind or an exacting imagination to create this world. Make the paper white, the ink black, yesterday's leftover bread stale, the stockings thrown over the chair back, having given up the ghost, the window transparent from rain, the sky grayish, and the land sinful. But maybe nothing worse happened than what you so feared. Even that little fool Psyche couldn't love in the dark her whole life. And it certainly wasn't the sisters' instigation that made her, on that last night, take a sharpened razor and a lamp filled to the top with oil to identify her secret husband, who was kind to the touch but invisible in the fortunate darkness. Alone now, she worries in her sorrow, although her decision has been made and her soul is adamant. Nonetheless she still wavers, rushes, delays, dares, trembles, despairs, rages, hates, and loves the darkness she has taken in, but evening is on its way to night, and the girl hastily hides the razor under her pillow and covers the burning lamp with a flowerpot. The final moments of anticipation. Agonizing, crazy-making moments that make her shudder. Suddenly the rustle of an approach. And now Psyche welcomes the night ascending to her—its shoulders and back scattered with freckles, like oatmeal. Coitus with the darkness. At last her mystery spouse falls still beside her, rolled up in a ball. Now Psyche, weakened in body and soul, rises, takes out the lamp, clasps the razor in her fist, takes a step, still not daring to look, and lifts the lamp, expecting to see on her bed a god or a beast—but it's you.

The day after classes ended, I stopped by the university vivarium, but they said Alexei Pavlovich wasn't there. I walked past the glass cases where white mice swarmed in trays. When I pulled one out by the tail, a whole cluster latched on. Their red eyes burned like cranberries. Frogs were laid up in huge, smelly jars, and the moment you opened a lid, one would fly out and land smack down on the brick floor.

A fish supper at home. They called for me. I locked myself in my room.

Daughter, up and at 'em. The surgeon's sturgeon's tired of waiting.

Eat without me, I'll eat later.

Zhenya, stop it.

I can't eat out there. He smacks his lips. Then he'll take a toothpick out of his pocket and dig around.

Why are you being like this?

Like what?

Enough, let's go.

Mika took the fish bones out for Roman, laid them on the rim, and the dish turned into a staring eye with off-white lashes.

You said: no letters. My naïve Alexei Pavlovich. You forgot about cartes postales. Not in vain did a bald professor at the Vienna Military Academy once drop the first postcard into a mailbox, paying for it with two Kreuzers and his entire soul. Ever since, the departed professor, taking on cardboard flesh, has languished around the world and found no rest. I found a whole pack of them neatly held by a rubber band in Vera Lvovna's writing desk. When you were away, you sent cards home daily with the sights and views, and—unintimidated by the censors—called your spouse your little mouse, your little bun, even your little fanny. Moreover, you always drew yourself in a picture: a stick man in a hat either roaming spectrally down the Samara embankment, or standing like a poet's shadow on the bluff of the Piatigorsk gap, or scrambling up the Admiralty spire like a gorilla. How, you might well ask yourself, can one resist such temptation, having fooled you and the postal department, of writing a postcard, an open letter, addressed at this late hour to all sleeping humanity? Here, please accept, from a place where this night cannot reach me, an unpretentious card with a glossy country landscape, gilt edging on the sunset clouds, a card scratched by swifts, splashed by a drop of a blossoming pond fragrant with lilac and iodine—it's my father, lost in conversation, whose bandaged finger keeps missing the point. Do you recognize our clumsy house, saturated with damp, permeated by mosquito buzzing, the sunny porch where a wet footprint vanishes instantly, the peeling barrel where the little bleakfish I'd caught were hidden away until October? When the barrel was emptied for the winter, the fish flopped all over the ground, sticking to the fallen leaves. And here, under the vaults of hundred-year-old lilacs, a windy June supper. Your wife is twirling the binoculars and laughing crazily, aiming them first at the moon, which has surfaced like a jellyfish, then at the deck chairs flapping in the wind, then directly at her plate. A pimply lass who arouses herself at night with her finger is eating the icing roses off the cake. I don't think that was me, but you know better. You're across from me. There's a whole beard in the rusty lilac inflorescences that drop on the table. You wink and mumble, "These are dead moths;" you scoop them up in your glass with a spoon and lick it off. My father—a cheap drunk—is shouting now, "I told them so. Here you are!" he shouted and brandished his empty glass. "Please be so kind as to join us! I'll cut their umbilicus. Congratulations on coming into the Divine light!" But they're shouting, they're not satisfied! They think, the Divine light is over there, while over here is the very Kingdom of Darkness.

Of course, my unclad little people, there's been a misunderstanding, you were misled, I explained to them, but there's nothing you can do. It's too late. Live as best you can! Here, my brothers, each has his own share of agony, his own path of suffering is marked out, and there's no avoiding it. Each must drink to the dregs! They strain and howl, as if to say, Why? We are innocently condemned! they say. And I tell them, Hush! You're all like this at first. But later? You don't honor your father and mother, you create idols, you commit adultery, you covet your neighbor's ass! So suffer and don't squawk! But again they holler! And wail!

When I came in, Alexei Pavlovich was wiping the dirt off the jars, disturbing the dissected popeyed creatures' peace.

Zhenya? Why are you here? Someone could stop by at any time.

Look at that, Alyosha,[9] you're afraid of me. I can tell. I was at your house yesterday. I went to see Vera Lvovna specifically because I knew you weren't home. I went to convince myself that she doesn't have long left. There'll be no need to hide, and this humiliation will end. We'll live

9 "Alyosha" is a diminutive of "Alexei."

openly, together, afraid of no one, and I'll give you a wonderful baby, scrumptious, chubby-cheeked, blowing bubbles from satisfaction when we tell him the bogeyman's coming to get him. My father will deliver the baby. He'll hold my hand and say, "Push, mama, push!" And everything will turn out well. I'll recover, I'll crunch a cucumber, and pale, tormented, and beautiful, I'll look down at you from my window, as you stand on the sidewalk under an umbrella, chilled to the bone, happy.

Zhenya, you have no idea what nonsense this is. You have to understand. This is vile, this is just plain vulgar, this is the height of banality—to cheat on a dying wife with a young idiot in love with love!

Yes yes, Alyosha, exactly so. A hymn to vulgarity. *Banalissimo*. Pistils and stamens. Life and death.

Quiet, Zhenya, I'm exhausted. Listen, tomorrow I'm taking Vera Lvovna south, to Yalta. For a month maybe. Or more. We'll see how it goes. You have to understand. Even when I talk to her about the weather, I feel like the worst scoundrel on earth! You know I'd leave her without a second thought, but how can I abandon someone in this situation? You don't understand. Some things are more important than love! Zhenya, my sweet Zhenya, we must part. Temporarily, of course. Vera says to me, "Where are you taking me? Why? What does it matter where I croak? Our friends are here, here Zhenya comes by." And I don't know what to tell her or how to explain. Well, why don't you say something? Say something quick, before they come in.

Bon voyage!

I was reading to Roman. Me in the armchair under the lamp, him on the couch. When the book was over, we sat in silence. I kept turning the lamp on, then off. What now? I mean, is the light on or is it dark? Not that that matters, Evgenia Dmitrievna, because I still hear you sitting.

I'm a nocturnal animal, you might say, Evgenia Dmitrievna, and we don't need light. One night I'll up and pounce on you. I'll sneak up and pounce.

It's been night for a long time, my kind Alexei Pavlovich, it's past two, and I wanted to sleep, but I can't, and my thoughts are all of you, or rather, of me—actually, they're one and the same. Can you hear the beetles droning in the fogged-up kill jar? Do you remember? You were lying in the spotty birch shade, covered with yesterday's newspaper, and sunspots and crooklegs were running across it. The fidgety daughter of your aging classmate, with whom you set out to assemble a collection for the dacha nature museum she'd just devised, was playing shaman around you, scooping up anything that flew, crawled, or stirred with her swift net. Having caught some pointless creature, the novice insectarian brought it over for identification. A piece of an article had imprinted itself on your wet forehead mirror-image. For a long time you examined the find under your magnifying glass, listened closely, eyes shut, to the droning in your fist, and finally announced, "Congratulations, child! This is the rarest stroke of luck! What a marvelous example of Dungus flyus." That was enough for this ninny to double up in the grass in fits of cascading girlish laughter. After she caught her breath, she badgered you about your wart: the girls had showed her a house where an old woman lived who bit off warts and licked the wound; she had some kind of special saliva. You were embarrassed and didn't know where to hide your hand. Later, on the cliff, she found a mighty, primordial swing: a very long rope with a stick at the end had been tied to a huge oak. There you were, sitting on a stump and reading a newspaper, though they'd long been expecting you for dinner, while the bundle of mischief swung and swung, and you, tearing yourself away from the letters, watched her rise up on tiptoe and clumsily pull up her foot to finally get one end of the bar under her, watched her freeze for a second, take a step, in the pose of a boy galloping on a pony, and then pull up her other leg, take a hop, lean way back, and fly off, spinning slowly, into the clouds.

I didn't go to classes and spent all day in bed. Early that morning my father came home from his shift. He was mumbling something, talking to himself, and he clattered his spoon in his glass for a long time. Then he went to bed. Mika got up and started checking on me with a thermometer, or milk, or drops of some kind or other. She tried to talk me into rubbing my legs and chest down with vodka. At last it was quiet: Mika took Roman to the professor's for his lesson, but before leaving she brought me a plate of apples. I snaked the apple peel spirals around my arms like damp bracelets. The boiler man stopped by to check the flue. He was just a minute, but the smell of wet, broken-down boots, cheap cigarettes, and green firewood lingered all day. My father got up. The crackle of fresh newspapers and the hot breath of borscht reached me. Mika and Roman came back from his lesson. Roman started tuning the piano, all the time repeating that the instrument was fine but very much neglected. He banged on the keys until I started pounding on the wall with an ivory knife handle. They quieted down. That evening my father and Mika went somewhere, and Roman paced around the apartment silently, feeling everything as he came to it. Only the old parquet creaked. That night I couldn't get to sleep, but on the other side of the wall they droned on. I was listening hard but could catch only snatches. Then I picked up a big glass flask that had roses in it, removed the flowers, poured the water into the chamber pot, and pressed the flask's bottom to the wall.

What are you trying to prove and to whom? There's no going into your place: you have a corpse peeking out of every nightstand. You're still young, healthy, and strong. No one would dare reproach you for anything.

You were a little boy then and you still are. You dug your heels in and stood counter to life, and you think you can hold out. But you'll be swept away. You've got this idea that Zhenya—it's as if she were her deceased mother and you were living for her. But that's wrong. You know nothing about your daughter. She's not yours anymore, she's her own person. You keep reaching for her to keep from drowning, but you don't have her anymore. Have you told Zhenya about her mother?

Mika and my father were silent for a long time, only I could hear the wet stems dripping from the edge of the table onto the floor. The ear I had pressed to the flask's neck was sweating.

When she came to us then she wasn't herself, I could tell right away. I asked, "Why didn't you bring little Zhenya?" And she said, "Leave me alone." I thought, Well, to hell with you. Living makes me sick even without you. If you don't want to tell me anything, you really don't have to. Then for some reason she stopped by at my neighbor's, a pharmacist. His little boy used to like all kinds of experiments, and his father had made him a laboratory. The lad started showing her his treasures. "If you drink from this test tube," he said, "you're a goner!" All this became clear later. In the middle of the night I suddenly woke up from a scream. I couldn't figure out what was going on because people don't scream like that. Then it was quiet. My Roman was breathing heavily, but she wasn't there. The bathroom door was locked from the inside. Behind the door there was some movement, shuffling, rustling. Scraping. I shouted to her, but she didn't respond. I wanted to give it a kick to make the latch give way, but then I looked and her fingers were reaching under the door. I shouted, "Your fingers, take back your fingers!" But they kept reaching. Somehow I got across the balcony to the bathroom window, broke the window, and nearly lost my grip, though it was only the second floor. I grabbed her and picked her up. She looked at me with horror in her eyes, she was trying to say something, but there was a jumble where her mouth should have been.

Evgenia Dmitrievna, thank God I'm blind, not legless, and there is no need to grab me by the arm and push me. I just need to hold onto your elbow. Like this. Let's go. And if you think that this makes me deeply unhappy, then you are mistaken, Evgenia Dmitrievna. I can see that you're unhappy. I can't see, of course, I said that wrong, though that's not something you can see with eyes, rather I can sense it. But you're not unhappy because you can't fly, for instance, or walk through solid objects, walls or earth. Isn't that so? I know you're afraid of me, Evgenia Dmitrievna. I mean, you think you pity me, but in fact you're afraid. Because it's yourself you pity, not me. Thinking about me, you imagine yourself in the dark, eyeless, and naturally for you this is scarier than dying. But the point is that blindness is a seeing person's concept. I live in a world where there is no light or dark, and that means there's nothing awful about it. My God, you should have warned me there was a sidewalk here.

God, prankster and coward, supreme lover, insatiable sperm-hurler, who each time chooses the guard for his fevered treasure on a whim—a bull-boor, swan-sneak—or sometimes you pierce me like sunlight—you're still a silly-billy. Remember how you kept dawdling and mumbling that you were afraid of hurting me? A god-child, even on a stolen bed, on that heavenly sheet, you wanted to be my obedient reflection, my pliant guide, and here you wanted to be my child. Here's Europa, straddling the horned monster, driving him on with her heels, Leda enveloping her flock with rustling wings, Danae grabbing the stiff but timid ray of light with both hands. A god-bungler, you tried to snatch everything on the fly, displaying your obscene zeal, and you became reckless, surfeited, pitiless, each time collecting your tribute more and more divinely, more and more lustfully. It was both frightening and thrilling to see the squinting, blood-filled bull's eye, to feel the swan feathers tickling my hips and the beak cropping the fragrant grass, and to see the golden rain twisting and turning as it spanked my belly and breast. Do you remember how you came to love the Mount Ida shepherd? The boy didn't suspect a thing, the boy with the rooster, or rather, chicken leg wrapped in a napkin so it was easy to hold; we took the other leg to the hospital. The child sat Turkish-fashion, poking the air with his knees; still wet, not chilled after bathing, he gnawed the leg, sucked the bone, crunched the cartilage, and his sharp little-boy shoulder blades, reflected successively in two mirrors and so seeming like someone else's, kept appearing and disappearing. Could this bird have flown past Ganymede? The naked adolescent jumped up, froze warily, not knowing whether to hide his nakedness from the eagle, still not understanding but already rigid from sensuous horror. The talons grabbed the boy's arm where his pockmarks were, squeezed, pierced them painfully, nearly broke the skin. Ganymede broke away, ran off, and tried to scream, but gasped for air: the mighty black wing fell on him and crushed him. Ganymede tried to beat it off, but his hands were twisted behind his back. Fear and sweetness mingled, the boy was afraid but simultaneously urged on this suppressed squawk, and the sharp bird tongue, wetting his ear, and the royal eagle talon, which had already groped out the road to the sky. Don't listen to me, my thinking pistil, know only that I love all of you, from your gray hair to the two hot hamsters squeezed in my hand.

I walked by a few times. Then I couldn't help myself and went up. I was just about to put the key in the lock when I thought I heard someone walking on the other side of the door. I was about to go away but thought better of it and rang.

So, you're Dmitry's daughter. Come in, don't just stand there. Alyosha told me, "Mama, I'm going to take my Verochka to the sea, but you can stay here for now. You never know what might happen." So here I stay. I think, who have I dressed up for, old woman that I am, got all made up for, put on my rubies for, set out the brandy for? I never expect visitors. Then all of a sudden—you. Drink up, sweet girl, drink a glass with an old woman, or else I'll go on drinking alone and reminiscing. Alyosha was very young when I said, "Eat your sausage, son!" He refused. Then I said, "Do you want me to make you a Maltese cross?" I cut off the sausage edges and fried it up. He ate it all and asked for more. "A Maltese cross!" he shouted. "A Maltese cross!" I said, "You're my nut, Alyosha! You're eating words, not sausage." What a happy one you are, sweet girl. You still don't know that you are me. You don't understand? No need. You wouldn't anyway. And by the time you do, I'll be gone—my skin, my hair, my eyes, my guts will be gone. And what's the use of bones alone?

I woke up and thought it was raining, but it was doves on the iron cornice.

Poor Mirra Alexandrovna decided I couldn't take a step without her. Here she was, torturing herself and me. But in fact, it's she who's helpless, not me. Getting oriented in the so-called visible dimension doesn't necessarily mean seeing. I assure you, Evgenia Dmitrievna, any blind person orients himself as well as you. That's not the main thing, you know, it's trivial. It's much easier than you think. After all, no two doors sound and no two rooms smell alike. Believe me, all it takes is a rustle, the creak of a floorboard, a cough, to know the size of the room, if it's a strange one, and whether anyone's in it, if it's your own. Empty and filled spaces sound different. It's easy to know when you're approaching objects by the reverse flow of air on your face, so it's absolutely impossible to run into a wall or a closed door. Evgenia Dmitrievna, I can immediately determine for you even a detail as small as whether a room is dusty or clean. Do you want me to tell you what you're seeing now? I just have to snap my fingers. Permit me. The curtains are drawn. The lamp over your bed is on—all it takes is holding your hand out to feel the warmth. There's a fresh newspaper and flowers on the table. Here there's an unmade bed. And the marvelous smell of perfume, eau de cologne, and lipstick is coming from over there. You're wearing a skirt but no blouse yet. It's reckless to change clothes in the presence of a blind man, Evgenia Dmitrievna.

What's happened to you, kind Alexei Pavlovich? I wouldn't recognize you. Where is your caution and prudence? How can you do such rash and risky things? It was a miracle your message didn't reach my father, since he always collects the mail. Only today, as if sensing something, out of the blue, I woke at daybreak and lay there for a long time listening to the wall clock and watching it swing on its stem toward the cupboard, but never quite all the way. Then some unconscious alarm, some inexplicable force, made me get up, get dressed, and go down for the mail. The clumps of snow—what the mailman left behind—still hadn't melted on the steps in the vestibule. I opened the box: papa's *Gazette,* some ads, and suddenly the Swallow's Nest floats from Crimea to the floor. Addressed in block letters, so he wouldn't recognize the handwriting, and instead of text, stamp-cancelled emptiness. Gasping from joy, I thought, but sensed with horror, that there was no happiness in this; on the contrary, the blank card held something humiliating, and I loved you in a completely different way. I put the newspaper and ads back, but I folded your little nest in two, slipped it in my pocket, and went back. Everyone was up by then. I think I wrote you before about Roman, the blind man and his mama dreaming of the conservatory. At the home where he used to live, it turns out, their favorite game was *gorodki*. One person sets up a figure, claps his hands, and runs back, while the other throws a bat. Remember that stuffed leopard cat in father's study? Roman touched it and said it was a squirrel. Outside, I stopped him for a minute and went to buy ice cream, but he kept talking to me the whole time—because of the street noise he hadn't realized he was standing there alone. He asked me to teach him chess, but he just couldn't remember the positions and kept running his fingers over the pieces. If the scissors weren't in the sideboard, he'd raise a scandal for his mother Mika—he calls her Mirra Alexandrovna. For that matter, he calls me Evgenia Dmitrievna instead of Zhenya. Mika came to me and asked me to put everything back where it was, and I explained that the position things happened to be in on the day of their arrival was by no means set in stone. I come home and lock myself into my room just so I won't see him. I can't stand to watch him constantly rubbing his stuck eyelids with his fist and digging snot out with a toothpick and licking it off. You can't go into the bathroom after him without a burning match. Mika brought us theater tickets. At the same time she laughed, turning to my father: "Every woman is a bit of a Traviata, isn't that so?" I spent half the day getting ready, but when it was time to go I still wasn't ready. Roman, sleek, wearing gleaming boots and smelling of Papa's cologne, was sitting in the hall by the door. Mika kept checking in on me every other minute. "Zhenya dear, let me help you! Zhenya, please, it's better to get there a little early and wait! Zhenya, how long can this go on? It's time! Zhenya, I beg of you!" I was all set when my coral necklace broke and the stone berries rolled all over the parquet. Mika waved her arms in panic. "Zhenya, just go, I'll pick them up!" I flew into a rage. "What do you mean just go! I can't go like this! I won't go anywhere like this!" I put on the lilac dress you like, or maybe you just said you did and really didn't notice, and now I wear it all the time. By the time we left it was obvious we'd be late. I said, "It's not so terrible. Imagine, we'll arrive for the second act. We'll have a nice walk, there's no rush now anyway. If Alfred sings his aria without us, he's not going to marry her because of it." Roman was giving me the silent treatment. After the rain there were puddles everywhere, and each one had to be stepped around or over. A simple, "Careful, there's a puddle," said nothing, and a few times Roman stepped right in the mud, splashing himself and me. He walked along pale and angry and didn't utter a word the whole way, while I chattered on. He stepped into a puddle again, stopped, and stated flatly he wasn't going anywhere looking like this. I said, "Don't be silly." He insisted. I couldn't restrain myself. "What earthly difference does it make to you what you look like!" A shudder ran through Roman, and he turned around and went home. I followed him. And so we returned in silence. Mika acted as though nothing had happened, as though it was all supposed to happen like that, but she wouldn't look in my direction. I also forgot to say I went to see your mother. She talked about what you were like as a child. I can just see it, the teary-eyed little boy running not to her but to me and telling me that the mean little boys there were catching baby birds, poking twigs through their eyes, and running around with these fluttering garlands, boasting over who had more.

Papa, are you busy? I wanted to ask you about one thing.

What, now?

All right, it doesn't matter. Later. Someday.

Naturally, Evgenia Dmitrievna, there are definite drawbacks to any situation. I don't like street orchestras. Drumming is to me what a thick fog is to you. Or a snowfall, for instance. Then it's like even the streetcar's wearing felt boots.

Or new shoes—that's a torture only the blind can understand. In general, as a result of their limited mobility, nonsee-ers' muscles are flaccid, their bones thinner, and their fingers—here, look—can be bent back without much effort. And I'll admit, I don't find the way you slip me thicker, sturdier dishes so I won't break them very nice, Evgenia Dmitrievna. On the other hand, believe me, the nonsee-er has his advantages. Why else would the philosophers of antiquity have blinded themselves? Evidently, they understood that your visible world, which you treasure so, is no more than tinsel, smoke, zilch. Those colour pictures say nothing about the essence of things; they only corrupt and render you helpless. With your eyes closed, you couldn't even get your spoon in your mouth. Of course, it's easy to cheat a blind person, but you can't fool him. It's not hard to artificially make the right facial expression in a conversation, but you can't do that with your voice. Words lie; the voice never. What seems important to you—colour, shapes, so-called beauty—are in fact of no importance whatsoever. Does it matter what colour the sky or wallpaper is? A bust that is usually admired is really nothing special—a head's a head. What difference does it make how you look, Evgenia Dmitrievna? I can't see you, but that doesn't change anything about our relationship. What difference does it make what kind of hair or nose you have? All that's important is that you hate me.

The floor polisher came and slid his brush under the couch and out rolled a dried up Christmas mandarin orange, ringing like a nut.

Zhenya dear, what's the date?

The teenth of Martober.

And they brought a blind man to Him, and they asked Him to touch him.

Taking the blind man by the hand, He led him out of the village, spat in his eyes, laid His hands upon him, and asked whether he saw anything. The man looked and said, "I see people passing by like trees." Then He laid His hands on his eyes again and told him to look again. And the man opened his eyes and saw everything clearly.

I explained, "Alyosha, my son, don't act crazy! Why should you marry her?" He said, "How can you not understand? Vera's having my baby!" I said, "Lord, who cares who's expecting what from who!" And he said, "Mama, what are you saying! What are you saying!" I always called her Vera dear, darling—but she bore me a grudge and set Alyosha against me. Right before the wedding, a miscarriage. "Alyosha," I told him, "This is a sign." My little idiot should have postponed the wedding and let everything run its course—to the end. But no, he married out of principle. "You don't love her," I told him. His whole body flinched. "How can you know whether I love her or not? On the other hand, I won't be a scoundrel." Then there was another miscarriage. That was right before my eyes. A five-month-old boy. Hands, feet, fingers, ears, wee-wee—just like a live baby. The third time they told her, Choose, it's either you or a child. What choice was there? For some reason Vera decided it was all my fault. That's ridiculous, of course, but in her condition she might have thought anything. I feel like a mother to her. I do understand... I sent them a gift at Christmas, a Chinese cup with a lid, the one I had from my grandmother. And what happened? I came home and my box was standing by the door. As if they'd said, Go choke on your gifts. You know, Zhenya dear, at the time, I remember, I went to bed and thought I could never get up. No, that's not it. I could, but I saw no point, no need. I wasn't even hungry. I lay like that a whole week. I'd eat a bite, wander around my room, and go back to bed. And then, you know, life won out.

It's all so simple. I laughed at myself, fool that I am. Life's like that, Zhenya. Afterward you have to laugh. Vera and I made our peace somehow. They would visit me on holidays, and I'd visit them. And here she's fallen ill, and I wanted to move in to look after. "Don't," she said. If she says don't, I won't. "Zhenya comes over, she helps," she said. "What Zhenya?" "Dmitry's, Alyosha's friend, his daughter. An odd girl, but good-hearted." And here you are. What a happy girl you are, Zhenya. The very best is just about to begin for you. I know. I had all that. Imagine, Zhenya, for me, after every time, a while later it would heal. Can you imagine? My doctor, the late Pyotr Ilich, was always amazed. "I can't tell you how many sugarplums I've seen in my day, but never in my life anything like this." That's what he called them, sugarplums.

So, kind Alexei Pavlovich, I hasten to inform you who is breathing seagull-beaten air that I had a fight with my father, that we made each other so mad we stooped to low blows. We shouted, trying to say the most hurtful things we could, and rejoiced in the wounds we inflicted on each other. I ran to my room and wailed for an hour. I assume you're already experiencing a slight incapacitation, an unpleasant chill: Did my father find out about me and you, about our plot, about the fact that I'm your secret, and therefore true, wife? Calm down. My father is still in the dark. What set us off was completely insignificant, not even worth mentioning. All that's important is that we are little by little, bit by bit, sucking the life out of each other, and the closer we are, the more lethal it gets. Mika came in with water and valerian drops and begged me to take them, but I waved her off, knocking the tray out of her hands, and the glass spilled on the bed. She said, "Zhenya, the bed has to be changed!" And I shouted at her, "There is no has to! Leave me in peace!" Here I am lying in the wet and writing these lines to you. You, kind Alexei Pavlovich, are afraid of my father.

So am I. I keep imagining telling him. What's scary isn't his anger, that he'd kill me and you—because he wouldn't—but something else. My father is irascible, crude, and crazy. But that's not why you're afraid of him. You're afraid because he's holy, not of this world. He's amazing, remarkable, a kind that no longer can or does exist. That woman, my mama, hasn't existed for a long time, she's absent in nature, and instead of her is a void easily filled by things and people, but my father has latched onto this void and won't let anyone or anything in. He thinks he's doing all this for me, out of love for me. He thinks he's living for his Zhenya's sake. He's never denied me a thing, neither money nor time. He could play with me for hours—puppets, theater, post office, all that childish nonsense. When I was just a child, he was already jealous of the whole world, even when I was simply playing with other children. It's a disease, insanity. He's not normal. You never know what to expect from him. He does impossible things. In the spring we went to Petersburg, and on the way back the train was held up at a station; some woman had thrown herself under the wheels. Everyone went to look, and I wanted to go, but my father wouldn't let me. I lay on my berth and read. Two Germans were standing by the open door in the passageway chatting. It was so stuffy, you couldn't close the compartment door. The train started. We rode and rode, and the Germans kept chatting, or rather, one spoke while the other listened. I already had a headache, and that voice was so grating and effeminate, I couldn't stand it. My father stuck his head out into the passage and asked them to move away or quiet down. I said, "They didn't understand you." And he replied, "The gentlemen are in Russia, so they should be so kind as to understand Russian." The German did not quiet down and kept chattering. Finally my father couldn't take it and hollered at him. "*Du, Arschloch! Halt's Maul!*"[10] The Germans cleared out.

10 "Shut up, you asshole!"

I laughed half the way home. When Vera Lvovna had just gone to the hospital, my father and I went to see her. After a thaw, there was sun, the way was impassable, and we could barely get through the mud. My father was hot, he was sweating, striding, his coat open. We bought oranges. I couldn't wait and ate one on the way and afterward my fingers were sticky. It was hot in the hospital, too. The heat was on, all the windows were sealed shut, and no one was airing the rooms out because they were afraid of drafts. On the ward, there was one withered old lady on one cot, and she was on the other, lying facing the wall. We sat down, my father on a chair, me on the edge of the bed. Without turning around, Vera Lvovna said, "This is it, Mitya,[11] this is it, this is it." My father cut her off. "Stop it! Those know-it-alls say all kinds of things." She turned around. Her face was tear-stained and swollen. "Vera, let me look at you." My father turned down the blanket, pulled her shift to her chin, and started palpating her breasts and feeling under her arms. Vera Lvovna lay with her eyes shut. "This doesn't mean a thing yet," my father said. "You'll see, everything will turn out fine." Then we ate the oranges. My father slit the peel with his Swiss knife and stripped it off, turning his nails yellow. The peel sprayed. I held one section at a time out to Vera Lvovna. When we left, the janitor on the corner was breaking up the melting ice. The splashes flew straight at us. My father shouted, "Have you gone blind or something?" The man waved his hand, as if to say, Get lost, removed his mitten and blew his nose. My father went up and kneed him in the groin. The janitor deflated and crumbled. I shouted and ran to my father, trying to pull him away, but he shook me off and punched at the man's cap from above so that the lout fell to the pavement. The ice, his face—it was all covered in blood. My father came to his senses and I led him away. His hands

11 "Mitya" is the diminutive of "Dmitry."

were shaking all the way home, and he kept begging my forgiveness. The day they did the operation, I arrived a little earlier, and there you were, waiting in a nook near the ER. We sat on a small wooden bench by a potted palm and watched the nurse move something from one cupboard to another. She must have been new; I recognized all the old ones. Then the nurse went away and the corridor was deserted. I took your hand and we embraced. That's how we sat, pressed close. Then the door opened and the nurse came in again. We should have moved apart, drawn back, let go, but that was utterly impossible, and we kept sitting with our arms around each other. The nurse said, "Young lady, let's go, you can help your mama. Don't worry so much. Everything's going to be fine." Then I stood up and went in.

P.S. In the room where Mika and Roman sleep, the door is opposite the windows. On a sunny day, beams stream through, jostling, and twisting around at the keyhole, and forcing their way into the dark hallway already twisted, draw on the opposite wall a miniature window hung upside down where, if you squat, you can see past the window frame and billowing curtain to the overturned roof of the next building over and the rusty top of a September birch lowered into the blue sky, like the fox tail from the story. Catch it, Zhenya, big and small. Now I was coming back from the bathroom without turning on the light, and I heard movement behind their bedroom door. I squatted and looked into that same keyhole, and Mika was there helping him beat off.

If you dream of your mother and she's alive, that means trouble; deceased, a change for the better.

I knew a woman I wanted to strangle, Evgenia Dmitrievna. I'd only just been taken home from the school for the blind. "Oh, you're blind! What a disaster! For long? Have you tried treatment? And there's nothing to be done?" And so on in that vein. "That's terrible, never to see the light! I'd rather die than be blind!" Or, "It's a pity you can't see. If you could, you'd understand." Her pity for me was quite sincere. I regret not killing her then because I don't think they put blind people in prison. But you don't pity me, so it's relaxing being with you. Evgenia Dmitrievna, you can't even imagine how grateful I am to you for that. Then, after I got home, for the first time in my life I truly felt like a cripple. You won't believe it, but among people just like me I was happy. The legless need to live with the legless, the blind with the blind. I had friends there and it was fun. Though you won't understand me anyway. Let alone our childish games. They tried to keep us as far away from the girls as possible, but you can't watch everyone. Nature takes its course, so to speak. What plays a bigger role for us than seeing people are smells. Now you smell like apple soap. I won't hide it. While you were gone I went around your room and sniffed your clothing, your dress, your underwear. So you see, at school I wanted to go home, but when I finally got home, I was suddenly unhappy. Just imagine. One day my mother was out and I ran away and got clear across town to the school myself. I don't know what I was thinking or hoping. It was an escape plain and simple. I ran away because it was nice there—no light and no dark, no blind and no seeing. Why I'm telling you all this I don't know. I love you, Evgenia Dmitrievna. Actually, that's meaningless. Goodnight.

Papa, tell me something about Mama.

Zhenya, I'm tired.

Tell me.

Tell you what?

Something.

What something?

I don't care.

Fine, tomorrow, I'm very tired.

Now.

What should I tell you about?

I don't know. Tell me about how when you were a student you climbed through the dacha window to see mama and her father clicked his nippers.

I already did.

Tell me again.

Zhenya, let me be.

No.

Fine, then. Your mama and her parents were staying at their dacha in Udelnaya. Zhenya, what's the point of this?

Keep going.

Her father had long nails. He called them nippers and was always clicking them. He was convinced, and tried to convince everyone, that the only help for mosquito bites was if you pressed a cross into the bite with your nail. He treated everyone. He was always trying to sink his nippers into my arm, too. After evening tea I said goodbye and headed for the station because the next day I was leaving for three months to do my stint as a medic at army training camp. Of course, I didn't go to the station, I went for a swim past the dam. The moment it grew dark, unbeknownst to anyone, I returned. The window was open. Her father was already asleep and her mother was spending the night in town. And that was the first time. The funniest thing was we didn't know what to do with the sheet. There wasn't much blood, but still. And the mosquitos were relentless. We lay there slapping each other. I said, "You can say you crushed a bloodsucking mosquito." She laughed. We never did think of anything.

The dawn came, I dressed, and I was about to jump from the windowsill. She whispered, "Wait a sec!" And she held out the crumpled sheet. On the windowsill was a glass jar of water with some kind of flowers. As I was jumping, my elbow knocked it over and it exploded like a bomb. At four in the morning. I leapt over the fence and ran for the station. Not ran, flew. And it was windy, too. I unfolded the sheet, held it over my head by the corners, and hollered for the whole neighborhood to hear, like a lunatic. "Hurrah! Follow me on the attack! Hurrah!" And the sheet flew overhead.

Here you are, Zhenya dear. But I guessed that if you came today everything would be fine. What exactly would be fine, I don't know. There's nothing I need, after all. I was like you and I wanted everything. Now I have and need nothing. Alyosha will be here soon with his Vera. He sent a telegram. They wanted to spend longer by the sea, but they only lasted a month. It's boring there. In the first half of the day, he wrote, they walked along the empty beach and fed the seagulls, and in the evening there was a touring midget theater. Here's what's funny. I was in Yalta a hundred years ago, and there were midgets then, too. But Vera keeps getting worse. She's capricious, has hysterics, makes scenes in public, and cries at night. He's had it with her. But what can he do? He has to be patient. She doesn't have long, after all. This is God's punishment for her, Zhenya dear. He punishes everyone and never lets anything slide. There's not going to any Judgment Day there. It all happens here. Zhenya, you don't even know how despicable she is. She cheated on Alyosha. I know everything. Alyosha was on an expedition in Central Asia catching some of his rodents. He asked Vera to come along, but she wanted no part of it, naturally. I was living with them then. Only a year had passed since the wedding. With Alyosha there she kept herself in check, but now it was bedlam.

She'd be getting ready to go out and suddenly shout, "Where's my button?" "You must have lost it somewhere, Verochka, and not noticed." "But when I came home all the buttons were there!" she said. I reassured her. "Life is funny that way. A button comes off and you don't notice." She shouted, "But I'm not crazy! All the buttons were there!" Is that supposed to mean I secretly cut off her lousy button? How many years have passed, yet when I think of that button, I shake with fury. I was supposed to go to Terioki for a rest then. I got to the station, boarded the train, went to get my ticket, and suddenly—Lord, have mercy—no wallet, no ticket, and there was a neat, very straight slit in my purse. I'd been robbed in the crowd at the station. Nothing to be done for it, so I went home. In the pouring rain, with my suitcase. I finally dragged myself there. I looked and there was an unfamiliar umbrella drying in the entry. A man's raincoat on a hook. It smelled odd, of some stranger, and there was also the smell of fresh nail polish. I listened: water splashing in the bathroom, and someone humming, a bass voice grunting. I opened the door to their bedroom, Alyosha's bedroom, and Vera was sitting naked in front of the pier-glass with her back to me, her foot resting on the base, polishing her nails. I coughed. She looked up and saw my reflection. I thought she'd cry out, get scared, start squirming and begging my forgiveness. But as if nothing were the matter, she dipped the brush in the bottle and went to smear the nails on her other foot. I said, "Why so quiet, Vera? Say something." I heard a splash from the bathroom. She replied, "What am I supposed to say?" "What do you mean?" I said. "I just left for the station and here you are… " She laughed. She was sitting with legs splayed, her big toenail red and the rest still bare. "Lord, who on earth are you?" She laughed. "Who? What makes you better than me?" I said, "What about Alyosha?" "What about Alyosha? This doesn't change anything. What am I supposed to do, jump out the window? If you tell him, he won't believe you anyway.

Leave and don't come back until tonight." So I left. I realized right away who it was in the bathroom, Zhenya. But I won't tell you. Why should I?

It's very simple, Evgenia Dmitrievna. Here's a ruler and a Braille board. One—open; two—close. You use this stylus to punch dots in the paper, but only Turkish-fashion, right to left. To read it, you take out the page, turn it over, and read it normally, left to right. Give me your hand. Feel it? One dot on top is A. Two dots one up and down is B. Two dots side by side is C. By the way, Braille also played music. All of Paris went to his concerts. He played cello and organ. But I have my exam in a week. If I end up failing, we'll be leaving you. I just feel sorry for Mirra Alexandrovna. For some reason she thinks I'm going to be a great musician. Poor, silly mama! I can't make her understand that the sensitive ear characteristic of every blind person isn't enough, that that sensitivity doesn't mean musical ability and true talent is as rare among the blind as among the seeing. I once heard my professor tell someone, "A pointless undertaking, doesn't have the hands or the feeling. But I'm still hatching. I have kids at home asking for food. I have three, dear." When we get home, I'm going to get a job as a piano tuner, that's good, too. If Fate smiles on me, I'll marry some kind blind girl. What else does happiness require? Normal young women only marry blind men in novels, Evgenia Dmitrievna. And if they do, it's out of ignorance. To tell you the truth, blind people are awful, Evgenia Dmitrievna. Spoiled, capricious, wronged, vindictive. The blind man's subordination in human contact is almost continuous; he doesn't choose his companion, who is whoever wants to be it. The constant dependence is humiliating and has a putrefying effect on the psyche. Egoism and vanity are the main motives for human actions; all that gets magnified exponentially for the blind. The blind man's vanity is fueled by the exaggerated admiration the seeing express for him out of pity for the cripple. The blind man is always in someone else's power, so he can't help but be suspicious, mistrustful, and vindictive. Marrying a blind man is like sacrificing yourself, only the sacrifice is thankless. People won't understand you anyway. They'll pity you and sympathize, as if you'd gone into a convent or become a nurse aide. And you won't be able to explain. So that everything's going to turn out just fine, Evgenia Dmitrievna. You'll see.

Zhenya dear, have you gone to bed? Are you asleep? Roman's going to play a little, just a little, all right? Please forgive us. His exam is soon, and that will be it. The professor said Roman has great talent, that he'll be a great success. He needs to work. He needs to study hard. Preparing for a performance is very difficult. He has to read the line with one hand and play with the other. Roman is very worried. He puts on a good face and pretends he doesn't care, but in fact he's afraid. If he doesn't get in, Zhenya, it will be a terrible blow for him. Not just a blow—a disaster. You do understand. In his position it is so important to find a place in life, to be essential to someone. Today I'm here, I'm always by his side, but tomorrow he's alone. How will he live? Who needs him? I think about this all the time, Zhenya. Lord, you look so much like your mama! You know, I should tell you one thing. It's silly, of course, not worth mentioning, and your dear mama's long gone, but I can't get the idea out of my head of how I deceived her. I mean, it wasn't really a deception, but still. She asked me to sew her a dress, and I promised. We came up with the idea together: a low back and a heart-shaped slit in front. Rustling taffeta with bell sleeves and a full ruffle. Imagine, chiffon ribbons from the fastening on the left and from the side seam on the right tied up in back in a bow. A dream, not a dress. She'd already bought everything: the taffeta, the buttons. I took the material home. You saw me off.

You were funny. You said, "Aunt Mika, bring me a wooly-booly!" I promised to bring the dress by her birthday. But I was having so much trouble with Roman, I never got around to the dress. There was never time. I kept putting it off. Of course, I didn't get it done, and it was time to go. I arrived, I was crying, and I lied that I only remembered on the train—I'd ironed the finished dress, folded it, and forgotten to pack it. She was so upset! Naturally, I would have finished the dress later, but that last time your mama turned up all of a sudden, without warning. She appeared on my doorstep and my first thought was, The dress! But she didn't remember. Something had happened between her and Dmitry. Or maybe nothing had, she just couldn't take it anymore. I don't know how she stood it all. They'd just got married, and he was already very strange. He wouldn't speak to her for days on end. He'd sit there looking at the wall. I asked, "What's the matter with him?" But this made her uncomfortable. She smiled and replied, "Pay no attention. Every person needs a wall sometimes." I didn't understand their marriage at all. They didn't know the first thing about each other. Your mother married him in a frenzy. One day she was trying to convince me that Dmitry was an animal, a lewd pig, a narcissistic nonentity, and the next she announced she was getting married. I said, "Are you out of your mind?" She shook her head. "Don't ask. I know nothing. And I don't want to." Mitya didn't just not love her, it was as if he were taking something out on her. Even having outsiders in the house didn't stop them. In my presence there were scenes between them at night that would end with Mitya taking the featherbed and going to the kitchen. She'd burst in and shout that she wouldn't let him treat her this way, that she was putting up with it for the child's sake, there was a limit to everything, and she would make him listen to her. But Mitya would interrupt her. "Pipe down, you'll wake Zhenya!" You would wake up and cry, and your father would pick you up. I would try to calm her down, but she was already hysterical. "You don't need me, I'm just in your way, you need the child, but you hate me! So know this. You won't have me or Zhenya!" I kept saying, "Leave him! This won't end well!" But she put up with it, she was waiting for something. At breakfast she would start poking her fork in the butter and could spend half an hour doing that, an hour. It occurred to me that she was quietly losing her mind. On my last visits her feelings toward you seemed to have changed. The slightest thing irritated her. The minute you acted up at the table, she'd start shouting, smacking you in the face, and pinching you so hard she'd leave bruises. You would cry, of course, and she would hit you even harder. "Quiet! Be quiet!" Then she'd clutch her head, cover her ears, and run away. One time you put on her hat, gloves, and shoes, draped yourself in her beads, took her rings, and smeared on her lipstick—and she lunged at you with a bamboo ski pole from your kiddie skis. We barely got her arms twisted behind her back that time.

I found out you'd arrived, my kind Alexei Pavlovich, and rushed off to the vivarium like a woman possessed. I made my way there as if sleepwalking, not myself, which was why I knew I was just about to see you, and suddenly a degenerate old cesspit of a woman approached me at a streetcar stop. She had blue prison tattoos on her arms and even her forehead. She wanted me to buy withered roses from her—lifted, obviously, from the statue of Gogol on the boulevard. "Buy them, girlie," she wheedled, "for good luck. You'll see, they'll come back to life." What did I do? I gave her a ruble, which the crone doubtless spent on drink, and immediately I felt that the witch, who stank of prison, had not in fact misled me and I was perfectly happy. Fool that I am, at that minute, at that stop, I would have happily died before the streetcar came. I stood and smiled, not in my right mind, and kept bringing the wilted fragrance to my nostrils and sniffing.

When I arrived, some people were there. You were angry, excited, not yourself. You were shouting that they were all idlers and thieves, that you couldn't leave for a minute, that you knew everything: they were feeding the dogs dog meat, and you knew where the meat allotted for them was going. For a long time you couldn't calm down, you kept snatching walnuts from the bag left over from the monkeys, squeezing three at a time, and the walnuts cracked, shooting off rotten dust. You started in again about how the nuts were dog shit, not nuts. Then someone came to see you and I slipped out because I didn't want to see you like that. They were drowning puppies there. Having nothing to do to keep me busy, I started helping. I'd pour water into the bucket, toss in the pups, and insert a second bucket into the first, also filled with water. I walked past the croaking jugs again for the umpteenth time, between the stands of trays where the white, sharp-clawed blobs bred faster than they could be done in. The dogs would quiet down and then the howling would start up from all the cages. Finally we were alone. I said, "Thanks for the postcard." You pretended you didn't know what I was talking about. "What postcard?" You held me in your arms and started kissing me. I asked whether you believed that we'd have to answer for all our actions on Judgment Day, and you said, "Let's go before someone else shows up." You pulled me by the arm, and we crawled into the farthest dog cage, where we put down straw. From directly above us came the barking of crazed canines trying to poke their snouts through the bars and sputtering spit. The sight of bloody cotton wool bothered you. You mumbled, "Zhenya, this can't be good." I objected, "It's fine." I reached under your shirt and ran my hands over your back and shoulders, feeling the tiny moles. You startled a few times—you kept thinking someone was coming. When they did come from the department to pick up frogs, you had a pleased look on your face, that you'd had time. I said in parting,

"I'm going to go to your house to pay Vera Lvovna a visit. Say hello for me." You mumbled, frightened, "Zhenya, I beg of you, don't. Don't come! I can't take it when you're together. It's awful for me." At home, at dinner, I upset the sauceboat by accident and it all spilled in Mika's lap. She jumped up, waved her arms around, wailed about how I'd ruined her suit on purpose because I always did everything to be mean, because God created me bad and ugly, with a face to stop a clock, and now here I was having my revenge for being an unattractive nobody. I said that Mika was trash because she wanted to marry my father and I was in the way. My father jumped up and slapped my cheek. I said, "I hate you all!" and ran out. I wanted ice cream but I had to make do with snow. Braille isn't nearly as clever as it seems at first glance. Here, this is about me and you:

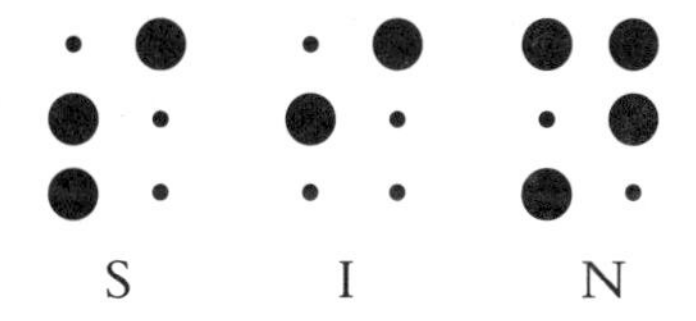

Zhenya, is that you? Alexei Pavlovich isn't here. How good you've come! I've missed you. This is just how it is, Zhenya. Healthy and pretty, everyone needed me, but I've grown fat and old, and now that I've got this horrible-looking face and missing parts as well, no one gives me the time of day. Don't think I'm hurt. What for? You weren't the one who thought this up and neither was I. We're not the first and we won't be the last. As if I haven't known for five years that one day they'd bury my body. In Yalta people kept asking me, "Why are you so cheerful?" I said, "Just look at that!" A magician there kept pulling a ribbon from his nose. I laughed till I dropped. They looked at me as if I were nuts. But I pitied them all for not laughing. They didn't think it was funny because they didn't understand something important. But I did.

Verochka Lvovna, tell me about my mama.

Your mama loved candy. Mitya brought her over to meet us, and I put a box of Viennese pralines on the table, a huge one, tub-size—and she ate half the box. But that's not the point, Zhenya. The point is that your father loved one woman very much. But she didn't. It happens. She liked it that way. She—how can I put this—toyed with him. It flattered her that he suffered so over her. She didn't even marry just anyone but his friend. And then when Mitya married the first girl to come along, he came to his senses. That happens, too, Zhenya. You'll see for yourself.

Verochka Lvovna, why are you lying?

Why indeed? You should always tell the truth. That woman was me, Zhenya. All those years your father and I would meet. And your mama knew about it. I told her all about it. But that namby-pamby, that Little Gray Neck, only whimpered. She asked, "What did I ever do to all of you? What?"

I'm going.

Go. Only listen to what else I have to say. In Yalta I realized why I'm not afraid. Everyone's afraid, but I'm not. Because I loved your father my whole life. I still do. I even wanted to write him about it. But I never did. Or rather, I sent a blank card. It's silly, of course. It never arrived, it got lost somewhere. I say this and I'm lying again because I'm afraid anyway. And also. You and Alexei Pavlovich could at least have waited until I croaked. Or do you think I don't see?

I don't care, Vera Lvovna. I don't believe in God and I smell of apple soap.

My handsome, intelligent, inimitable, delightful, prickly, unlucky Alexei Pavlovich, by the power of imagination invested in me I'll make you who you are because I want to. Your hair is falling out, tufts of it get left in your comb.

Your skin is getting flabby and wrinkled. You're developing a soft, almost feminine belly. After four flights of stairs now you have to catch your breath. You can't see close up, you're afraid of glasses, and you read holding the book at arm's length. Your soiled and chalk-stained jacket hanging on a nail in the classroom by the board automatically spreads its sun-light-reflecting elbows. In the bathroom I scrub your mangled name off the walls. You're ordinary and not that smart. Remember how we started telling our fortunes out of boredom? Your page, my line. We got: "But whoso shall offend one of these little ones which believe in me, it were better for him that a millstone were hanged about his neck, and that he were drowned in the depth of the sea." You said, "We'll find a rope, but where are we going to get the stone?" I made-believe I was tightening a noose and stuck my tongue out to the side. We burst out laughing. You and I. You're a silly man. After all, I was the one who needed the millstone. You were one of the little ones. And now, like a foolish child, you think someone's angry at you for something, but you don't understand what, and you're lost in speculation as to why people avoid you, you're looking for explanations, seeking out meetings, even writing notes that really don't become you. You're ridiculous and repulsive both. You pulled an underhanded trick, announcing loudly in front of everyone that I should come by your lab after the lecture. I came and became the unwilling heroine of an extremely vulgar scene. I didn't even realize at first that you were asking my forgiveness for the row of our lesser brothers preserved in alcohol with their guts hanging out. You started trying to convince me that you still loved me and that the lack of attention and caresses was simply out of sensible caution because no one should know anything before it was time. "We have to keep a low profile, Zhenya," you explained. "You have to be patient." I said all I needed was purity and I left. As it turned out, you didn't understand anything. And now this awful yesterday.

Or maybe, on the contrary, you did understand and that's why it all happened like that. Kind Alexei Pavlovich, do you even remember what happened? You showed up at my father's birthday totally drunk. You wouldn't let anyone get a word in and badgered everyone about what a remarkable father and worthy man he was and poured yourself shot after shot. You pestered Roman to play. The poor boy didn't know where to hide, but you sat next to him, put your arm around him, and wouldn't let him go. You shouted in his ear, "Roman, do you think you're the blind musician? Silly! It's him!" He lifted a forkful of herring toward the ceiling and the sauce dripped down his fingers into his sleeve. "Him! He pounds on us like keys, like this and this!" Mika jumped up. "What are you talking about! You don't even know what you're babbling!" I went to my room and lay down so I wouldn't have to see or hear you. You knocked on the door. I thought it was my father, but it was you. You collapsed to your knees and started kissing my feet and exclaiming that you couldn't go on like this, that you would throw her on the garbage heap, that you had no one and nothing in life but me. I said, "Go away! Get out!" You kept trying to kiss me and I kicked you away. You fell to the floor. They ran into the room. My father dragged you to the front door. You were laughing, trying to break away, and repeating over and over, "Thinking pistil! Thinking pistil!"

There is a famous phenomenon, recovered sight, Evgenia Dmitrievna, described back in the eighteenth century. Someone blind from birth who acquires vision after an operation thinks that the objects he sees are touching his eyes. He can't judge distance and misses when he tries to grab a door knob. They show him a sphere and a cube. But he can only tell what they are by feeling them. Amusing, isn't it?

Here I am writing you one last letter, kind Alexei Pavlovich, which, like the ones before, you will never receive. Any novel, no matter how short, should have an epilogue. Nothing happened, it's just that your Zhenya changed. This different Zhenya came home one fine day and found a tear-stained Mika sitting there. Zhenya asked, "What happened?" Silly question. Zhenya knew full well that Roman had taken the exam and failed. Zhenya stood by the window in her room for a while, watching the little boys in the courtyard taking turns blowing into an empty bottle, and then she went into Roman's room. He was sitting like a statue. Zhenya started reassuring him and said that it didn't matter, it was all silly, because that wasn't what was most important. "What's most important," Zhenya said, "is that I love you. I'll be your wife, we'll go away from here, and we'll just live." She started kissing his face, eyelids, and forehead, but he had a fever. They took his temperature—he was burning up. They put him to bed. They called the doctor without waiting for my father. Pneumonia. How? Why? Mika and I sat with him that night, together. Roman mumbled something in his fever. Then fell asleep. Zhenya asked, "You don't believe me?" Mika answered, "I do. Roman loves you very much, Zhenechka. And I know that you can make him happy. Only I'm afraid you'll bring him grief." But Zhenya said, "Whether you believe me or not, I love your son and I'll do everything I can to make things good for him. If only you knew how happy I am right now!" Zhenya sat at his bedside day and night, spoon-fed him, gave him his medicine, sponged off his sweating body, changed his sheets, and took him to the bathroom. She and Mika discussed what kind of wedding they would have. Zhenya wanted it all to be very quiet—first church and straight home, and there only their closest friends and a simple supper. "Yes yes, Zhenya dear," Mika agreed. "We'll do everything your way."

How frightening to wake up without you here, Evgenia Dmitrievna. Here I am holding your hand, and I still can't believe it's true. My beloved, my one and only Zhenya, how well you put it then: we'll get there and just live. You'll be my better half, my spare rib, my God-bestowed wife, and I'll stuff myself on pears.

Before going to the train station, we all sat quietly for a minute. The streetcar outside set the bookcase glass to shaking.

You got all the way downstairs and had to go back.

"The gingerbread! We forgot the gingerbread!"

Cottonwood puffs swept even through the front door.

We arrived at the station early; they'd just brought the train up.

My father flicked a puff off his sweaty face and shielded himself from the sun with a newspaper.

Quickly, get in quickly, it's about to move, any minute now. The train sailed past the Andronikov Monastery, whipped by the oncoming wind.

Would you like me to tell you what's out the window right now? Can't you feel it when the knocking of the wheels changes? First we were going over an embankment, now we're in a hollow. Going down and down. Look, what did I tell you? A tunnel."

At a station where we waited an hour, a garbage can was smoking.

You can feel the heat subsiding. Zhenya, Roman, let's have dinner. In the morning we'll be home.

The paperclip Roman used to mark his place in his book had gone missing.

Where are you going, Zhenya? It's only a five-minute stop.

I'm going to stretch my legs. Don't worry, I have time.

They were selling cherries and steaming potatoes on the platform. Out of a big kettle, so when the lid was lifted, steam spilled out.

Mika poked her head out the window, waved, and smiled.

Zhenya, it's time. Or you'll be left behind.

It's all right, Aunt Mika, there's still time.

The train blew its whistle and was enveloped in steam like a potato. The cars jerked in a chain. Slowly, Mika started moving.

Zhenya, what does this mean? Zhenya, how can this be?

The suitcases, Aunt Mika! Send my suitcases!

What about Roman? How could you? How could you?

She returned the next morning, but she didn't go home. She went there.

She opened up with the same key. It was dark in the entry. She turned on the light. Hanging on the coatrack was the same coat with the mother of pearl buttons. She grabbed one and pulled hard. The button flew apart. She tore another off, taking fabric with it.

Alexei Pavlovich came out of the bathroom with bare, wet arms.

Zhenya? What happened? Vera Lvovna's here washing... What's the matter with you?

Everything's fine. There is no light or dark.

What?

Let's go.

She took him by the hand and led him into his room.

What's wrong with you?

She fell on the bed.

Something heavy slapped on the bathroom floor.

She held him tightly, squeezed him with all her might, held her palms hard to his shuddering, bumpy back.

She began to laugh, drinking in life.

Translated by Marian Schwartz

Language Saved

When I arrived in the city of Joyce for the first time, I went straight from the train station to the Fluntern cemetery. The streetcar was full to the last stop. Everyone got off at the cemetery and headed with me down the path between the gravestones in the direction indicated by the arrow: "To James Joyce." I felt uneasy. The closer we got to Joyce's grave, the more numerous the procession became. The burial site was surrounded by an already packed crowd—and on a work day, not an anniversary of any kind.

I had always assumed that the author of *Ulysses* was more respected in the West than in my homeland, but this...

Shaken, I looked for some catch, only to find it immediately, unfortunately. They were burying Elias Canetti, who had asked to be laid to rest alongside the great blind man.

Canetti begins *Tongue Set Free* (whose original title could also be rendered as "Language Saved") with his first childhood memory. At two, someone frightened him (his nanny's lover, as would become clear many years later), by rapping his penknife and joking villainously, "And now we'll cut out his tongue!" The fear of being rendered tongueless would pursue the child, adolescent, youth, and writer for many years. His whole life.

I experienced something similar when I saw the generously daubed backdrop of the Alps. The fear of being left tongueless. Swiss German clanged all around me.

Later, everything fell into place.

Actually, it was quite simple: I had to set my own language free so that my language could save me. I began writing my novel all over again, but in a different way and about something else.

It had just become more obvious that I had to write purely and clearly.

One expects a highly inflected language such as Russian to come in twos, like livestock or people, and to count off: one-two, one-two; translate this, don't translate that. Moreover, in translation, what can be translated doesn't so much get translated as mutate.

Say any word, the most inoffensive, the most objective, for instance, "scholarship," and misunderstanding immediately sets in. It is one thing for a scholar *here* to study agricultural relations in the fifteenth century in the Canton of Glarus, where five hundred years later the land still belongs to the same family. It is quite another to talk about private ownership of land *there,* where that kind of scholarship is fuel to the fire of a future civil war.

So it is for any word in the dictionary.

The experience of a language and the life lived through it turns languages with different pasts into noncommunicating vessels. The past that lives in words does not yield to translation, especially that Russian past which was never a fact but always an argument in the endless war the nation has waged against itself.

Each word individually and all words taken together only exacerbate the impossibility of interlingual understanding and horizontal communication.

Ever since the Tower of Babel, the task of language has been to misunderstand.

The art of Russian speech has its own bottled up aroma, ingredients inherent only to the substance of Russian literature. The story of Bloom's first and last day can be translated into Russian, but Joyce's text rejects our national language's substance. The words' blood curdles. There can only be a "Russian Ulysses" with a "little man's soul" à la Leskov.

The students in the Zurich Slavic seminar read Kharms (with a dictionary and delight), but it's not the same Kharms. The Swiss Kharms is about something else. Ours is Platonov's identical twin. Their words, their Russian substance, cast on the Alpine wind, are pure and clear.

The absurd of OBERIU—the Russian Futurists' Association of Real Art—is an extension of Akaky Akakievich realism in a country where war and throwing old women out windows is simply a way of life. The most absurd and Kharmsian text cannot help but become the very megaphone through which old women squawk before slamming into the pavement.

This is a healthy disease; you can live with it until you die. Its causes rest partly in genetic predisposition, partly in birth trauma.

You have only to cast an eye over the stages in the great journey of our nation's chicken-scratches. First came the epaulets, ribbons, and odes on ascension. After plodding along for not very long, Russian letters retired, basically. It read at its leisure and, when it had recovered its sight, it swelled from a sense of its own importance. And wrapped itself up toga-fashion in Gogol's overcoat. Henceforth and ever after, Pushkin's seraph from his famous poem "Prophet" would lie in wait in some vacant lot or on the Swallow Hills, where Herzen and Ogarev made their famous vow to each other, and crush the balls of anyone writing in Russian, twist his arms behind his back, rip out the fleshy organ that delivers food to the teeth, as Dal's dictionary defines it, and whisper: Rise up, see, hear, and burn!

In line with his era's tastes and the stench of circumstances, a prophet can reveal himself anywhere, even to hardened convicts stashing novels under plank beds, the way poets did trying to survive the Gulag. And this can in no way alter his status: what a seraph gives only a seraph can take away.

Not even the most vomitous language of the most vomitous era, even the most absurd method for describing reality, the most exquisite pen craft, can change anything in the relationship between someone writing in Russian and the six-winged, who themselves have been sent by someone.

One can think only of how words taste, but no matter how hard you try, you cannot violate the job description. Thus, nature has thought of everything: man thinks about the delightful rubbing of genitalia and the result is children. A prophet thinks about the delightful turning of the tongue and a seraph gives Cyrillic its essence, meaning, spirit, and depth. Kharms wrote about old women falling out of windows and the result was the end of the world and the sole possibility for salvation: to love and repent.

But horizontal communications are impossible even within a single language. Even speaking Russian, there is no understanding one another. Yurovsky reads out the sentence in the Ekaterinburg basement where the tsar's family has been assembled, but Dr. Botkin doesn't understand, just as Pasternak and Khrushchev misunderstood each other—or the person standing outside with a sign against the Chechen war and the general populace. And what about on a crowded bus? Or in a marital bed grown cold?

How does one give language the purity and clarity needed for understanding? This has nothing to do with being tongue-tied.

A tied tongue, starting with "she sells seashells," proceeding through a lead article on enemies of the people, and moving on to Brodsky, is actually language's sole possible form of existence. Refined literature is just another way to be tongue-tied.

One simply has to find a tongue tied in just the right way to explain something. To say something and be understood.

How correct the reception is depends on how correct the code. But everything in language is necessarily aimed at confusing the code and complicating understanding; from the beginning, language has put up an infinite number of boundaries and limitations and introduced utter mayhem.

The search for a code of understanding ties the tongue on a whole new level. Boundaries narrow and walls rise swiftly. The space for understanding collapses and leads to its logical conclusion.

For whom was *Finnegan's Wake* actually written? Robert Walser spent his last writing decade on novel after novel, his handwriting tinier and tinier, as he and his letters moved off into infinity.

If the point of language is still communication, then communication between whom?

In what language did St. Francis and the birds communicate? Or rather, better to ask: with whom was the barefoot man from Assisi whistling back and forth?

Intel's boss once said that he could never outdo the Creator and man would always be the universe's best chip.

A processor is dead without animating code. A user has to have software to establish contact with the hardware.

A human being released into the world is given a tongue so that he can have vertical communication.

Something has to transform the burning thickets of thorns—every summer forests do burn—into a burning bush.

For mortals, language is the User's sole form of existence. Thus, it represents both creature and Creator simultaneously.

Walser would have been surprised at the reproach over the indecipherability of the letters he wrote, letters which toward the end of his life shrank to the size of a period. Joyce had no doubt about the intelligibility of *Finnegan's Wake.* Both said what they wanted to say purely and clearly, and they were understood.

"And then they did take the hermit priest, the monk ascetic, Epiphanius the elder, and did cut his tongue out whole; from his hand they did sever four fingers. And in the beginning he spoke in a nasal voice, and then he did pray to the Virgin Mother of God, and shown to him were both tongues, the one of Moscow and the one of these parts, in the air; and he, taking hold of one, put his own in his mouth and ever since began speaking purely and clearly, and his tongue took root in his mouth and lived."

Translated by Marian Schwartz

Nabokov's Inkblot

I stood in the arrivals terminal of the Zurich International Airport, holding a sign with the name KOVALEV and feeling happy.

Our son wasn't even a year old and my wife was at home with him. Meanwhile, I couldn't seem to find a steady job. Life was hard in those days and we had to scrimp on everything. It was sufficiently demeaning that I couldn't earn enough money for my family, and on top of that we had two birthdays coming up—first my son's, then my wife's. I desperately needed money for gifts. I wanted to buy my loved ones something wonderful and special, or maybe whisk them away on vacation somewhere; do something, in short, to make them happy. But there wasn't even enough money to pay the rent. And then luck struck: I got a call from the interpreter agency. They needed me to meet a client at the airport, drive him to the hotel, then the bank, then to Montreux. So that's how I ended up standing in the airport, enjoying life. Aside from the promise of good pay, I was especially excited that the trip would take me to an extremely important place for me—to Nabokov. The client had reserved the very same room at the Montreux Palace where the writer had lived, so even the lowly interpreter would have a chance to visit that sacred place, the dream of any Russian reader. I waited for the delayed flight with my sign and daydreamed about how I would sit at *his* desk, open the drawer, and finally see the famous inkblot that I'd read so much about. Nabokov's inkblot!

I'd be able to touch it with my fingers! Joy!

Then I saw Kovalev. I recognized him immediately. And he, of course, did not recognize me. I hadn't even thought that this could be the same Kovalev. Of all the Kovalevs in the world!

My first crazy thought was to thrust the sign into his hands, turn around, and leave.

But his wife and daughter were with him. The girl was around five years old; she smiled at me and handed me a penguin, the stuffed toy she carried with her on the plane. I didn't know what to do with it, but it turned out that I was only supposed to make his acquaintance. The penguin's name was Pinga.

So instead of leaving, I shook hands with Kovalev and started saying everything that's expected in such a situation, things like "Welcome to Zurich! How was your flight?" and so on.

We drove to the Baur-Au-Lac, the hotel where they were staying.

In the taxi, Kovalev kept trying to work out some sort of urgent problems on two cell phones at once and in his short breaks engaged me in conversation.

He had emphatic opinions on every subject.

"Swiss Air has really let itself go! The flight was late and service was horrendous!"

Or, "Those Alps are nothing. You should see our Altai Mountains!"

Or, "The Swiss are so good-natured only because nobody's kicked their ass in two hundred years!"

As the lowly accompanying interpreter, I didn't argue. They paid me by the hour.

I remembered Kovalev as a skinny blond kid wearing a Komsomol pin that nobody else bothered to wear, and that he, too, took off when he left the Institute each day. But now, here he was, a "New Russian" in an expensive suit, complete with a stately paunch and premature bald spot.

At one point we were students together at the Moscow State Pedagogical Institute, I in the German department and he in the English department, two grades above me. He was a Komsomol official and gave speeches at faculty meetings and school assemblies. They loved Kovalev in the administration because he announced the decisions of the Party congress in a pleasant voice, as if they were joyful revelations, and we hated him for it. After finishing at the Institute, he stayed on the Komsomol line in the capitol's district committee. It was clear; a guy like him would go far in that life. I despised him.

Life was completely different now, but Kovalev still ended up on top. And I ended up on the bottom.

Kovalev didn't even think to use my services as an interpreter—at the hotel he checked in using fluent English and headed to the bank for his meetings, sending me off on a walk around Zurich with his wife and daughter. My former classmate quickly made it clear that he was paying for a lackey, not an interpreter. He was obviously convinced that his high status made him deserving of such service.

Kovalev's wife's name was Alina. A wife like that was also guaranteed for someone of Kovalev's status; she was young, beautiful, and, of course, blond. And the stroll around Zurich was also appropriate for her high class—she bought only the more expensive things in the boutiques on the Bahnhofstrasse. Yanochka, the daughter, was bored with shopping, so I amused her with conversations about penguins.

"Did you know," she asked, "that penguins love their children so much that they don't eat anything at all for half a year while they warm their baby's egg so it doesn't get cold?"

"Yeah, I think I've seen something like that on TV," I answered. "And I think it's actually the father penguin who sits on the egg."

"Really?"Yanochka wondered. I think this increased her pride in her own father. "My daddy buys me anything at all that I want! And also he promised me that I could ride a pony!"

It seemed like Alina had been to Zurich before, because in the end she was leading me around the stores instead of the other way around. I gloomily trailed along behind with her purchases. Then we sat in the Sprüngli café where Alina told me that she was a former athlete who used to do rhythmic gymnastics. I could tell from her figure. It seemed like she wanted someone to talk to, and I found out that her dream was to work as a trainer, but that her husband wanted her to stay at home with the child. And then she started telling me about how good a father Kovalev was, how much he loved Yanochka, absolutely doted on her!

I stared at Alina, trying to understand. Did she really love him or had she simply made an advantageous marriage? She didn't give the impression of a dumb blond, and she actually seemed to love Kovalev.

"To be honest, I can't stand shopping," she admitted suddenly. "I just have to get presents for some acquaintances and I'm always afraid I'll forget someone."

And as a parting gesture she even told me a joke:

"Two New Russians meet in Zurich on the Bahnhofstrasse. One shows the other a tie: 'Look! I bought this at that stand for two thousand francs!' And the other says: 'You're such an idiot! I saw the exact same tie at that other stand for three thousand!'"

She burst out in happy, youthful laughter. Pinga waved goodbye with his wing, or maybe his flipper, and we parted until morning—the next day I was to go with them to Montreux.

That night our son didn't fall asleep for a long time, cried, and had a fever. My wife sang him the lullaby her mother used to sing for her.

Schlaf Chindli, schlaf
De Vater hüetet d Schaaf
D Mueter schütlet s Boimeli
Da falled abe troimeli
Schlaf Chindli, schlaf

I couldn't sleep either, so I lay awake and listened to her lullaby and my son's light wheezing. These were the two most important people on earth, and I really needed a job, urgently needed to get money for them. I wanted my son too to be able to say someday:

"My daddy buys me anything at all that I want!"

But I had no money and still couldn't find real work, getting by on these chance jobs instead. There was also the fear that my wife was secretly asking her parents for money. I was ashamed. Just a jobless *Ausländer*. A poor foreigner in a rich country.

The child finally fell asleep and my wife lay down and pressed up against me, but I still couldn't sleep.

"So, tell me what's wrong," she said. "I can feel that something's bothering you. Come on, love, tell me about it. We're together; what can be so bad?"

I told her about Kovalev, how, many years ago, he was a lackey to the regime, and how I despised him.

"If we had met somewhere by chance, I wouldn't have even given him my hand to shake. But here he is with this pile of money from who-knows-where—and I'm his lackey."

"You're not a lackey. You're earning money. Doing honest work, that's all. Any job can be done with dignity."

"You know," I said, "money smells everywhere, but in different countries it has different odors. In Switzerland, money masks its smell with deodorant, but in Russia, money reeks. Petty cash stinks like poverty, but big money stinks like dirt, crime, theft, bribery, deception, and blood. Big money can't be honest there. Where do you think Kovalev got all that money? You don't make that kind of money in Russia in ten lifetimes through honest labor. And now he comes here with his bag of dirty money and opens a bank account. And I get a cut of the action. Here I am, earning his filthy money with my 'honest labor' as a lackey! And I'm supposed to do this with dignity!"

She said, "Love, don't do it! Turn it down, then. To hell with the money! But go to sleep now, it's so late."

The next day I headed to Montreux with my clients.

On the way, Kovalev shared more of his views on the world:

"They've put up all this radar on the autobahn, and they're so scared. You don't even really live your lives here, you're too afraid."

Or:

"Why do the Swiss need an army? How many billions for a couple of airplanes so that someone can fly around over the Alps as much as they want? You have so much money here you don't know what to do with it!"

Or:

"Now Nabokov—he was a genius. All of these modern writers are shit!"

My former acquaintance's passion for Nabokov didn't fit with either his Komsomol past or his Big Business present. But I didn't ask him about it. Because what an idiotic question—why does a person admire Nabokov?

But still, it was strange. When we were young, Nabokov was banned. You had to copy him out by hand, type him out on the typewriter. We passed him along secretly to one another and thought of ourselves as a persecuted sect, his books our treasured riches. No, maybe we felt like a battalion at war—because there was a war on, a war of the system against our minds and souls. And Nabokov was more than a writer; he was our weapon.

Reading was more than a way to pass the time out of boredom, but a fight, a defense. We didn't want to be slaves and defended the only morsel of freedom in that life—our heads. Nabokov was our symbol in those years. Nabokov marked the dividing line between Us and Them. Kovalev was definitely a part of Them. And now he was driving me to Montreux. Everything was so strange...

The little girl got carsick and we had to stop several times. Kovalev moved to the back to sit with his daughter and started to distract her with different stories. He thought up fairy tales in which the main character, played by Yanochka, was always landing in the hands of bandits or dragons and battling her way out. The Yanochka in the fairy tale always won. She listened intently, not smiling.

It was February. Moscow was still in the midst of a blizzard, but in Montreux spring had already begun, the sun beat down from the sky, and seagulls flew lightly and playfully over the mirror-like lake.

The famous quay was not yet black then from Muslim burkas—instead it was full of neat old ladies in furs and sunglasses taking their daily walks. Kovalev unzipped his coat and squinted in the direction of the Alps, blue in the haze:

"Yeah, this is just how I imagined everything would be!"

I had to take endless photographs of him with his wife and child at every corner.

When Kovalev registered at the Montreux-Palace, he questioned the girl behind the counter suspiciously to make sure he really was given the same room where Nabokov had lived. The affirmative answer did not satisfy him, and he asked again when the bearded bellboy wheeled the suitcases into the hotel room. The bellboy also assured Kovalev that he was not being tricked. The bellboy turned out to be from Serbia. The Americans were bombing Belgrade and blood had only very recently been spilled in Yugoslavia, so the Serb, having heard Russian being spoken, refused to take his tip out of gratitude to Russia—and immediately received twice as large a tip. Kovalev and the bellboy even hugged.

Kovalev was disappointed with Nabokov's room. I explained to him that after Vera's death everything had been remodeled, and the writer's space had been divided into separate rooms; but he was appalled by the crooked low ceilings, narrow windows, and tiny balcony.

"How could he stand to live here?"

Old photographs of Nabokov hung on the walls of the room, and Kovalev wanted to recreate each one. He called room service to request a chess set and sat down at a table on the balcony with Alina, just like Nabokov with his Vera. He made me take lots of replicas.

Of course, Kovalev also wanted to have a picture of himself behind Nabokov's desk. For the first time, I was glad Nabokov was dead.

When Kovalev and his wife went out to the balcony, I opened the treasured drawer—the memorial inkblot, the one I had once read about, the one I had dreamed about touching for so many years, was right where it was supposed to be. I touched it lightly with my finger. I don't know what I was trying to discover but Yanochka prevented me from doing it. She ran up and peered into the drawer.

"What's that? Show me!"

"Here, look!" I said. "The inkblot."

She was surprised and obviously disappointed.

"An inkblot..."

Kovalev said the room was too small, and they ended up staying in another room, a giant one.

They put me up in the hotel next to the train station for two days.

First thing in Montreux, I had to look for a pony. After all, Kovalev had promised Yanochka a pony. Kovalev and his wife stayed behind in their hotel room, while Yanochka and I set off to ride a pony. The little horse was sad and smelled terrible.

Yanochka was keen on me for some reason and didn't want to say goodbye, so the Kovalevs invited me over for dinner. At the table, Kovalev was either in raptures over the beauty of Lake Geneva and Swiss cleanliness and order, or else he expressed dissatisfaction: the hotel's sauna was not properly heated, security at the entrance was lax—an invitation to any old person off the street if he isn't lazy—and most importantly—you trip over Russians on every step! For some reason the abundance of his compatriots bothered him most of all.

I was amazed at how lovingly Alina looked at her husband. You can't fake eyes like that.

The riddle of Eva Braun. How can women sincerely love criminals, crooks, and ruffians? Will anybody ever be able to explain this?

Maybe it was animal instinct? The male's place within the herd does determine the survival of his offspring. The most cruel and devious ones become the leaders and wield the power, so their children have a better chance of survival. Women want to bear the children of leaders, of alpha-males who give them and their offspring protection. Maybe that's it?

Or maybe everything is simpler: a woman doesn't fall in love with a criminal, but with a man, with the vitality and strength he exudes. She falls in love with his force of life.

At dessert Kovalev declared, "How can you live here? It's so boring! Are you even living here? You're just rotting away!"

I was eating on his dime and had to agree with everything.

"Here, in the West," he said, chewing with pleasure, "people are so miserly, putting everything off until tomorrow. But back home in Russia, people are greedy with life. Because if you don't take something from life right now, tomorrow there might not be anything left!"

He did everything greedily—ate greedily, laughed greedily, sucked the air coming off the lake greedily into his nostrils. He even took photographs greedily. Nothing was enough for him.

But more than anything, Kovalev loved taking pictures with his daughter. It seemed like he sincerely loved her a lot. He called her "bunny," which was distasteful for me because that's what we called our son—"bunny."

That night I tossed and turned in my bed at the train station hotel. I couldn't sleep out of self-hatred. Was I really jealous of this guy? Why was he the one staying in Nabokov's room and not me? I'm the one who loves Nabokov. I'm the one who was saved by his books, banned long ago in our homeland. For some reason I had always thought that if I were able to touch that sacred inkblot, I would understand something very important, very deep. And now I had touched it—and what did I understand? What was the revelation?

I lay there, listening to the occasional late train pass, and the same miserable thoughts kept crawling into my head: why can Kovalev afford to spoil his wife and daughter while I have to play lackey to his rich family, just so I can get some money for my son's and wife's presents from this impossibly smug guy? Who is he? How did he get his money? Was he a better student than I was at the Institute? In that late Soviet era life, when you could make the choice between a small debasement—to be quiet—and a large one—to give speeches—he voluntary chose the large one. In any country, at any time, there is always a minimum level of immorality necessary to survive. But it's possible to stop at that level. Though maybe it's not, if you actually want to accomplish something in this life. I was certain that in the new epoch he was still choosing the larger debasement, disgrace, dishonor, in order to get even richer. I suddenly imagined that tomorrow morning I would tell him all of this right to his face and then leave. And only then did I fall asleep.

But the next day I drove them on an excursion to Chillon castle and was friendly, talkative, and attentive. I was gathering material for my *Russian Switzerland* and probably made a pretty good guide—I told them all about the Russian crowd in Chillon, sprinkling in amusing quotations.

I couldn't stand myself, but I knew why I was doing it.

Russians are familiar with a particular kind of conversation: train talk. Strangers meet each other in a train car and spend a day, two days, three days in a cramped compartment together. And then they part forever. You might spill out your soul to a random traveling companion, tell him things that you'd never tell friends in your daily life. On that evening, our last evening together, we had one of those train talks.

Alina went to put her daughter to sleep, while Kovalev and I sat at the hotel bar, and he ordered a bottle of the most expensive cognac. It was unlikely that Kovalev was interested in me as a conversational companion; he probably just needed a witness to the causal manner in which he ordered the bottle, which cost the average monthly salary of a cashier at Migros Supermarket.

We drank. The cognac was actually outstanding.

I remember I told him a funny story about how Nabokov and Solzhenitsyn, two giants of Russian literature, never met in the Montreux Palace Hotel. They wrote to each other and agreed to meet: Nabokov wrote in his daybook: "6 October, 11:00 Solzhenitsyn and wife." Apparently Solzhenitsyn was waiting for a letter confirming the date. He came to Montreux with his wife Natalia, walked up to the hotel, but decided to drive on, thinking that Nabokov was either sick or for some reason didn't want to see them. Meanwhile, the Nabokovs waited for their guests at the restaurant for an entire hour—without ordering lunch—not understanding why they weren't showing up. After that, they never ended up meeting.

Kovalev shrugged his shoulders. I guess he didn't think the story was funny.

Then we drank some more, and he suddenly smiled crookedly.

"I thought your face looked familiar right away, but I just couldn't remember where I had seen you. Have we bumped into each other before?"

I assured him that, no, we hadn't.

Alina called and said that she would stay in with Yanochka.

Kovalev started asking me about how I ended up in Switzerland, about my Swiss wife.

"Aren't you bored among all these flowers and chocolates?"

He drank more than I did and quickly began to get drunk. Out of nowhere he started telling me about how his first wife was a bitch and how happy he was when they divorced.

"I came out of the courthouse and felt like I was flying! I swore I would never get married again. I kept my word for five years and then Alinka came along! I love my Alinka like a madman! How could you not love a woman like that? Have you seen her body? Tell me, have you?"

He had a revolting habit of slapping his companion first on the knee, then on the shoulder.

"And I love my Yanochka so much that I'd do anything for her! You believe me?"

I kept nodding my head the whole time. That was enough for him.

We sat there for a long time. In any case, one bottle wasn't enough and he started ordering himself more shots.

Kovalev told me something muffled and unclear about his business, about the criminals he had to deal with, about how disgusting it was for him to take part in all this filth, and how he was doing it all only for Alina and Yanochka.

"See," he yelled so loudly that everyone in the bar kept turning around to look at us, "I don't have anything on this earth as dear as Yanochka! I'd kill anybody for her sake! If he so much as touches her with one finger! I'll do everything for her! I'll become a murderer myself! I'll stuff my face with shit! I'd do everything for her, for my bunny! Got it?"

And then he whispered confidingly in my ear that he had ensured a future in Switzerland for his wife and daughter in case something were to happen to him.

"You never know," he explained. "Anything could happen. But I did everything so that Yanochka can grow up here. Among all the flowers and chocolates! I've fixed it so that everything's provided!"

When he was totally wasted, he started to confess that his enemies were out to kill him.

"See, I'm already a marked man! And I know it! And I know who!"

I think he didn't really understand where he was and who he was talking to. He drunkenly growled, "But I won't let them get me! I'll hang onto life by my teeth, see? By my teeth!"

We left the bar and went outside to get some fresh air down by the lake.

We stood on the waterfront. We couldn't see the mountains in the fog and it felt like we were standing at the edge of a great sea.

Kovalev yelled out to the whole Lake Leman in the night.

"You think they marked me alone for death? No, they marked all of us! All! And you too, understand? No, you don't understand shit! You have to live now! Maybe this lake won't even be here tomorrow!"

I smirked. "So where's it going to go?"

He waved me away with his arm. "You didn't fucking understand anything!" and trudged back to the hotel on unsteady legs.

But I spent some more time walking along the waterfront. I felt like I was drunk, like I was talking to myself. The rare passersby turned to look at me. I told myself, "What if something happens to you? He ensured a life for his wife and child—you didn't. You despise him, but how are you any better than he is?"

And then I felt very sharply that the lake might not in fact exist tomorrow.

The next morning, we said our goodbyes. Kovalev seemed crumpled. His eyes were red and glazed. He looked at me strangely, with a heavy and unpleasant stare.

"Yesterday I might've blabbed a little too much—forget it! Got it?"

I nodded.

The tip I got from Kovalev was fit for a king. In a good movie I would leave his money on the table and proudly walk out. But we were not in a movie.

Alina and I said goodbye almost like friends, and Yanochka just hung on to me and wouldn't let go.

We didn't see each other after that.

On her birthday, my wife unwrapped the boxes of presents. I badly needed to hear her laugh happily, to see how our son smiled from his bed.

Having your loved ones near you is the only important thing, and everything else has little meaning.

One morning a couple of months later I sat down at my computer and on the Yandex newsfeed I stumbled upon a familiar last name. Kovalev, one of the executives of a well-known bank, had been shot to death on the street right in front of his building. Just a typical news story for Moscow at that time.

The killer had waited for the victim next to the entrance lobby and fired an extra shot at his head to be safe—the neighbors saw this from their windows.

I don't know what happened to his wife and daughter. So many years have passed. Yanochka has to be so grown up by now. I wonder what she's like today. Who did she become? What happened to her life after the death of her father? She must have grown up somewhere around here, in Switzerland.

What if you're here now, reading this, Yanochka? The strangest things can happen in life…

I wonder what you have left in your memory about our trip? Maybe everything's been erased, besides the pony? How's Pinga doing? He's probably long gone by now.

And what do you remember about your father?

He would've explained to you himself about our Institute, and about everything else. And about why he was killed.

Or maybe he wouldn't have.

You know, the only important thing is that there was a person for whom you were the most important being in world. Everything else is inconsequential.

Tell me, do you remember that inkblot?

Translated by Mariya Bashkatova

Of Saucepans and Star-Showers

All winter long I fantasized about spending the summer in Valais and roaming the mountains every day. I pored over the map and plotted out various routes. I'd be mountain-bound bright and early and homeward-bound come evening, tired and happy after a full day's ramble.

But then summer came, and I landed up in hospital with a bilateral hernia. There was no escaping postoperative complications, either—inflammation, high fever, antibiotics. As soon as my stitches were out I went off to Brentschen. But I had to kiss goodbye to all my wonderful plans. No hours-long hikes in the mountains. The first few days I ventured only as far as the table on the lawn in front of the chalet. I gazed at the Weisshorn and rejoiced at life.

The mountains in this vicinity have inspired so many descriptions that they seemed like quotations emerging suddenly from beyond the clouds.

I thought, too, about how, as the years go by, taking genuine delight in something becomes possible only when you can share that delight with somebody else. My son had promised to come and visit for a couple of days, and, watching the Rhône valley change colour in the twilight, almost as if it were pulling on a lilac stocking, I so wished I could enjoy this spectacle in his company rather than alone.

But he could never seem to find the time to come.

As I waited for his visit, I gradually started getting out and about, venturing further and further from the village each day, now taking the level road towards Jeizinen, now the mountain track in the direction of Leukerbad, and every time I imagined how we'd stroll around these parts together. I walked at a leisurely pace, often stopping. The stitches itched unbearably—I wanted to pick the plaster off and tear at the scars with my nails.

Then my son emailed to let me know he was already on his way. His short message ended with the following riddle: imagine a saucepan big enough to hold anything you like—a chicken, a whole bull, a house, the entire Earth, even the entire universe. Yet what can such a saucepan never hold?

Let me explain. The thing is, his mother and I divorced when he was seven. I became a pop-in father. And, later, a fly-in father. Things were probably better that way, for everybody and for him first and foremost. When his mother and I fought—undignifiedly, inanely, smashing crockery and slamming doors—he didn't cry, just threw himself now at her, now at me, his hands clenched into little fists. Living like this was impossible. My leaving home did us—my son and myself—a world of good. Had we continued to live together, I would have only shouted at him: put your shoes away! Or, Do your homework! Or, Stop badgering me, can't you see I'm writing! But because I'd left, our get-togethers throughout his childhood were about him and for him only, and I never told him to stop badgering me. Not a single time. It was worth leaving home for that alone.

In periods away from one another we'd exchange letters. About anything and everything. I thought up various charades for him, crosswords, riddles. In each letter he'd pose tricky questions of his own, such as: If steam is lighter than water, then why is ice not heavier than water, but lighter?

He's all grown-up now, but he still rounded off that email with one of his riddles.

He's twenty-three now, an adult.

By the age of sixteen I already knew everything about myself. I knew what I wanted from this life: to write books and to travel. And I knew that this was impossible. Because I was born into a country where whatever I might write would never be published, and beyond whose borders I would never be allowed to travel. This was a slave-country, and my slave-parents had birthed me into bondage. I knew exactly what I wanted, but it was all impossible—and I felt like a disconsolate wretch.

My son, in contrast, has it all within his grasp: he's already travelled half the world, he writes, makes films, gives concerts of his own music. But he still doesn't truly know what he wants from this life. Which makes him feel wretched, too.

Happiness, most likely, is conditional neither on liberty nor on its lack.

There I was, strolling along the track in the direction of Leukerbad, the air laden with the sharp aromas of the warm sunlit forest, of pine resin and wild strawberries, and I pondered what it was that wouldn't fit into a saucepan big enough to hold the Milky Way, all the galaxies, and the entire universe from beginning to end?

And then I encountered my father. He was walking towards me, a rucksack on his shoulders, sturdy mountain boots on his feet, sunbronzed, healthy, young. This was my father, but not as I knew him in his final years, a grey-haired, gnarly guzzler. This was the father I remembered from my childhood. I stopped, astounded, while he strode over to me, nimbly and vigorously, as does a weary traveler at the conclusion of a whole day spent on mountain paths, with the end of a long, splendid hike finally in sight.

Drawing level with me, he smiled and said, "*Grüezi!*"

"*Grüezi!*" I replied.

And he strode on towards Brentschen.

The fact that my father had spoken to me in Swiss German brought me back to reality. Needless to say, this young man, many years my junior, could not be my father, delivered to the flames of a Moscow crematorium in his sailor's uniform seventeen years previously.

During the war my father had been a submariner in the Baltic, and a photograph of his Shchuka hung on our wall. That Daddy had a submarine was a source of great pride for me as a child, and I'd constantly be making drawings of the photo in my school exercise book, carefully inscribing the number Shch-310 on the submarine's nose. Every ninth of May—Victory Day—my father would get out his sailor's uniform, which he was always having altered to accommodate his ever-growing belly, and pinned on all his badges. Later I grew up a bit and realized that in 1944 and 1945 my father helped sink German ships which were evacuating refugees from Riga and Tallinn. Hundreds if not thousands of people met their deaths in the waters of the Baltic—for which my father was decorated. I've long since ceased being proud of him, but nor do I condemn him. There was a war on, and my father won in that war. He was avenging his brother.

My father went off to war as a volunteer at the age of eighteen—to avenge Boris, he would tell me. His older brother was killed in the summer of 1941.

As a child I'd spend every summer at my grandmother's, in the holiday village of Udelnaya near Moscow. A wall in her room was hung with old photos. One showed her sons: two teenage brothers sitting in embrace, head to head, floppy ears touching. Nowadays everyone always smiles on photos, but these two gazed seriously into the camera as if they had foreknowledge of everything that would soon happen to them.

Another snapshot showed a youth in headphones: a ham-radio aficionado, Boris was training to be a telephonist.

I remember Grandma unfolding the frayed old sheet of paper marked "NOTIFICATION," kissing it and wiping away tears. He was twenty. Looking at my son today, I find this simply impossible to imagine. He's just a boy still, no more than a kid. But back then, Boris seemed like a big grown-up hero to me.

My grandfather was a peasant from down Tambov way. He was arrested in the midst of collectivization in 1930. Grandma would tell me about how, when requisitioners arrived at their yard to take away the cow, he became indignant at being left with nothing to feed two little children. He was arrested and sent off to Siberia to build the Baikal–Amur Mainline. He managed to pass on two short letters before vanishing. When Grandma was dying, aged ninety-five, her mind started going a bit, and everything that happened to her in 1930 began resurfacing. I'd phone her, I remember, and at first she'd speak to me as normal, but then she'd suddenly start asking, "Who is this? Misha? Who's Misha?" And I'd tell her, "It's me, Misha!" Her husband, my grandfather, was also called Mikhail, and she'd scream down the phone, "What are you doing? Leave him be! Don't take him away! Let him go! Misha, where are they taking you?" She had been transported back to that year, and her husband was being arrested all over again. To avoid dying of hunger, Grandma had to flee the village with her two children, my father and Uncle Borya. She found a job as a cleaner near Moscow before spending the rest of her life as a kindergarten nurse.

On every form he filled out, my father held back the fact that he was the son of an enemy of the people, and he lived his whole life in fear that this would come out into the open. It's so important for a son to be proud of his father. But it was fear, not pride, that dwelt in my father's soul.

That frayed and yellowed document Grandma kissed and cried over wasn't actually a notice of death, but a notification that Boris was missing in action somewhere in the Kandalaksha area. Such an odd word that it stuck in my memory. This is a small town in Karelia. Now I realize she was forever hoping that he hadn't perished, that he was still alive somewhere. "Missing in action"—what does this mean, exactly? Could mean anything. And she thought, What if he's still alive, what if we're to meet again? And my father harboured the same hope about his brother.

Grandma died in '93, my father in '95. And then, in 2010, something happened—the sort of thing that normally happens in films or books, not in real life. I was in Norway. A translation of my novel *Maidenhair* had been released there, and I was invited on a tour of speaking engagements across several cities. My Norwegian translator Marit Bjerkeng and I were strolling around Tromsø, a town in the country's far north, and we popped into the small local museum. Two diminutive rooms housed an exhibition about Soviet POWs in Norway during the war years. The retreating Germans evacuated their camps from Finland to the Tromsø region. And all of a sudden I remembered that word from my childhood—Kandalaksha. That was where the notification had come from! Kandalaksha was somewhere in Karelia. And I thought, what if my Uncle Borya had been captured there, and was then transferred to Norway in 1944 together with the other prisoners? Marit helped me make an enquiry to the Norwegian archives. A copy of the registration card of POW Boris Shishkin was found immediately and sent to me by email.

POW'S PERSONAL CARD. ISSUED AUGUST 29, 1941. STALAG 309. All their camps were called Stalag—a contraction of Stammlager. This number designated a network of camps in Finland. Every POW was given a metal ID tag, and his number was 1249. SHISHKIN, BORIS. BORN DECEMBER 30, 1920, IN THE VILLAGE OF NOVO-YURIEVO. NATIONALITY: RUSSIAN.

PRIVATE, MILITARY UNIT NUMBER. CIVILIAN PROFESSION: RADIO-MECHANIC. TAKEN CAPTIVE AUGUST 27. IN GOOD HEALTH. FINGERPRINT. SURNAME AND ADDRESS OF KIN IN POW'S COUNTRY OF ORIGIN. MOTHER: LYUBOV SHISHKINA—my grandmother.

Reading this, I came into a sharp realization of what it was to be resurrected from the dead. This person, my twenty-year-old uncle, now thirty-three years my junior—this boy had suddenly come back to life! And it hurt so much that neither my grandmother nor my father had lived to see this day.

I went straight off to the Internet, and you can find everything there, including information on this Stammlager 309. Photographs, investigations, documents. Stories of people who were imprisoned there and survived. There were even photographs of firing-squad executions taken on the sly by a German soldier. POWs were predominantly employed in construction—they built railways. I read about POW telephonists—and realized: of course, that was him! He must have been given work within his profession!

On the reverse of the card was a note: ES BESTEHT DIE VERMUTUNG, DASS DER KRIEGSGEFANGENE JUDE IST, LAUT AUSSAGEN EINES VERTRAUTEN MANNES. WURDE AM 25.7.1942 DER SICHERHEITSPOLIZEI ÜBERGEBEN. Which means he was shot.

In the course of my Internet research on Stalag 309 I came across a photograph of executed POWs in a big pit. Perhaps one of them was my father's brother.

How can I convey this feeling? My uncle Borya has just been resurrected—and he's been killed again. It's a good thing after all, I remember thinking, that Dad and Grandma didn't live to see this!

That he was killed as a Jew is, of course, astonishing. He was of Tambov peasant stock, going back generations. Evidently someone had got square with him: the slightest denunciation might get you shot.

I set about tracking down that photograph from my childhood. Our family archive was destroyed ten years ago when my brother's house near Moscow burnt down. I got in contact with my father's last wife, Zinaida Vasilievna, but after moving house numerous times she had nothing left. It's extraordinary: I see it right before my eyes, that prewar snap of the youth in headphones, but it exists nowhere except within me.

Every document, every photograph, everything that should be kept in the family from generation to generation—it has all perished. But it all still survives in what remains of that machine of death. Why? How on earth can this be?

I was also struck that a Russian translation had been written onto the card in someone's hand. Who did the translation? What for? When? There was a Russian stamp, too: PERSONAL REGISTRATION CARD AMENDED. REFERENCE NUMBER 452. 1941. And a handwritten word: NOTIFIED. Meaning that Boris's mother, my grandmother, had been sent the paper she was to cry over for so many years.

It turned out that all these archives were transferred to Russia after the war and are held to this day in Podolsk, near Moscow. My grandmother and my father lived so many years in ignorance of their Boris's fate, and it was their own country, for whose sake Boris had died, that held the truth back from them. Only after Perestroika were the archives opened temporarily, and Western historians made copies of them. I received Uncle Borya's card from the Norwegian archives within a single week, yet Grandma and Dad received no news of him from their own state in a whole lifetime.

Information concerning POWs was kept secret because in reality the state was waging war against its own people. My relatives, my loved ones lived out their entire lives in a prison nation which used them for its wars and despised them.

When Perestroika began, my father made an enquiry to the KGB about the fate of his father. All the victims of Stalin's repressions were being rehabilitated. He showed me an official letter confirming the rehabilitation of his father, my grandfather. Charges were being dismissed for lack of *corpus delicti*. Dad had been tanking up since morning and would only bellow, "Bastards! Bastards!"

After the war he drank his whole life through. And all his submariner friends, too. They probably couldn't do otherwise. It was the disease of their generation. Aged eighteen, he spent months on end immured in a submarine, haunted by the constant fear of drowning in an iron coffin. An experience like that can shackle you for the rest of your life.

Under Gorbachev, when the really hungry years began, my veteran father received food parcels containing produce from Germany. In his eyes this represented a personal humiliation. He and his friends had seen themselves as victors their whole lives, and now he was forced to feed from the hand of the vanquished foe. He regarded the collapse of the USSR as defeat in a war he had waged together with the rest of the country. My father hated Gorbachev.

I didn't like Gorbachev either, but precisely for the reason that he did everything in his power to prevent the collapse of the USSR and the entire Soviet system. My father and I viewed the history being made around us from opposite vantage points. There was an unbridgeable gulf between us. We had long since ceased to be close to one another. And this, of course, had little to do with politics.

The final straw leading to our estrangement came at my wedding. Inviting him, I remember, was a conciliatory gesture on my part. Dad got drunk, started a punch-up, and I had to restrain him with the help of a friend and pack him off home in a taxi. It was hard for me to forgive him such things.

It's so important to be proud of one's father. But I was ashamed of mine.

I started communicating with him again only shortly before his death. He spent his last years simply destroying himself with vodka. Denied his drink, he'd start smashing up everything in the house. Zinaida Vasilievna stopped fighting for him—she herself would buy him his bottles so he'd get sozzled and quickly pass out. He drank so much it seemed strange his body was still holding up. All his submariner friends had long since drunk themselves into the grave. My father must've been in a hurry to rejoin his war buddies. Out of their whole boat he was the last man standing.

At the funeral feast Zinaida Vasilievna told of how my father died:

"He's fallen off the bed and he yells, 'Zina! Zina, I can't see anything! Turn the light on! The light! I need more light!' It is light, Pasha, I say, it's sunny outside!"

It was odd that my bibulous veteran-submariner father should have uttered the same dying cry as Goethe.

For as long as I can remember, my father always said that, upon his death, he must be laid in the coffin wearing his sailor's uniform. And at the morgue a grey-haired swabby was wheeled out to us in an open coffin. Lately his whole body had been quaking and shaking, but now, arms folded on his chest, he had an air of serenity, as if mollified by the thought that he wasn't being cremated just any-old-how, but in his striped sailor's jersey.

The coffin turned out to be too short. His head wouldn't fit—it was wedged up against the coffin wall, his chin pressing into his chest—and his face wore a strange, lively expression which betrayed mild annoyance. Can't even put me into the coffin properly, it seemed to be saying.

Zinaida Vasilievna went off to remonstrate with the morgue authorities, but they just jabbed a finger at the receipt: You ordered 180 cm, we put him in 180 cm. A woman in a grubby white coat and rubber gloves came out and started explaining that coffins must be ordered with room to spare because dead bodies tend to stretch:

"Were you unaware of that or what?"

Zinaida Vasilievna waved a hand, loath to get involved:

"Do whatever you want! I've no strength left to deal with this."

We had to go to the crematorium at Mitino. A bus was laid on, caked with dirt to the very windows. I made to close the coffin. Nails had already been hammered into the lid, but I only noticed this when it wouldn't shut properly. I took a look: a nail had lodged itself right into the top of my father's head. Something reddish-blue had oozed out of the ripped skin and into his grey hair. The coffin was left open.

As I sat in that screechy, clapped-out bus—clutching the seat for fear of being sent flying by a pothole, my leg keeping the coffin from sliding away—I remembered the bike rides to Ilyinsky Forest Dad and I went on every August before school started. Time and again he'd shoot off ahead on his heavy trophy cycle. "Dad, wait!" I'd yell, and I'd try and catch him up on my Orlyonok, hop-skipping over tree-roots: there were pines all around, and weaving along the paths would've been better. At times you'd come across sandy areas, and your tires would sink.

In the crematorium, when the time had come to close the coffin, I bent the nail to the side as best as I could so Dad would be spared more pain.

Shortly before he died, my father resolved to have us photographed together.

"What for?" I said.

He tried to convince me:

"I'll pop my clogs, Mishka, and you'll look at the photo and maybe you'll think back to your old man the sailor!"

"All right, old-man-the-sailor, let's go!" I said, just to get him off my back.

We went to a photo-studio near their house just outside Strogino. We sat down in front of a Lumière-brothers-era camera. The photographer, a young girl with a boyish hairdo, said, pulling a strand of gum from between her teeth, "You could do with a smile!"

Our attempt to produce one couldn't have been too convincing: "Say cheese, now!" laughed the girl.

Just recently I was looking for something or other, going through old papers, and suddenly there it was—that very photo. Dad and I, earlobes touching, both with cheese in our mouths.

My son phoned in the evening, when he was changing trains in Brig, and I drove down in my old Golf to pick him up at the station in Leuk.

He came out of the train with a massive backpack—that's how he travels the world. We hugged. Every time I see him these days, I marvel at how grown-up he's become—a whole head taller than me now.

On the way back I pestered him with silly pointless questions about his studies, about university, about his flatmates. He studies in Vienna. *Historisch-Kulturwissenschaftliche Europaforschung.* He told me about his amusing professors, whom he loves for their love of history, and I listened enviously. I studied foreign languages at the Lenin Pedagogical Institute, but the principal subjects there were history of the Communist Party and scientific communism. And I hated the professors. How strange that slavery should be known as a science.

While he took a shower and unpacked, I got supper ready: fried potatoes with onion and sausages.

"Mmm, smells good!" he shouted from his room.

We ate at the table by the window, looking on as the Weisshorn glowed pinker and pinker in the sunset. *Alpenglühen.* I told him about my encounter with my father on the mountain path.

"I barely remember Granddad. Tell me something about him! What can you remember from your childhood?"

And I started telling him about what I could still recall. About how, when he was drunk, my father would always start belting out the 60s hit "Mishka, Mishka, Where's Your Smile?" and, wrapping his great big arms around me, a preschooler, he'd make me sing along, but I tried to struggle free—his drunken stench was horrible. And about how we'd go cycling in Ilyinsky Forest. And about other odds and ends. Suddenly it transpired that the long years of my childhood had been distilled into a mere handful of recollections.

One involved a trick my ex-submariner had once shown me. I see it clearly: we're going for a haircut on a Sunday, and I'm whingeing—I'm scared of the hair-clipper and I hate the barber's. He's pulling me by the arm, and look, he says, look at this trick! And, miraculously, Dad's become a giant, and he's holding out on his palm a tram that's pulled in to a stop.

My son laughed and said that I'd shown him that same trick when he was a kid. Only it wasn't a tram I had on my palm, but the high-riser on Vosstaniya Square.

We started reminiscing about his own childhood. About how we went off to meet his mum at the station one day, and it was so heaving with people we were scared we'd lose her, and then I sat him on my shoulders, and he saw her and yelled at the top of his lungs, "Mummy, mummy! We're here!"—and was dead proud later on because he thought that, had he not spied his mum out in the crowd from the height of my shoulders, she'd never have found us.

"Tell me," he asked, "what's the happiest childhood memory you have of your father?"

I remembered the haymow. Born in the countryside and into a peasant family, my father lived his whole life the wrong way—as a city-dweller, spending years in some office—but he yearned to be a peasant, to work the land that had been taken away from them. And so, come summertime in the dacha, he loved working with the soil, planting apple trees, crafting, digging, building. He always dreamt of sleeping outside, on a haymow, rather than in the house. Once he brought a whole haycock over from somewhere and fixed himself a bed right under the open sky. I was about seven or eight, and I cajoled him into letting me sleep with him. It was such a delight to lie on that prickly bed, nuzzling into my father's shoulder and breathing in the overwhelming fragrance of the hay! It being August, stars were falling. We lay there, the universe looming above us, and looked on as meteors streaked across the sky.

We sat and talked, my son and I, until it was completely dark and the stars had risen over the Valais. And suddenly he said, "Let's go!"

It was cool outside now. We wrapped ourselves in blankets and settled down into armchairs on the lawn in front of the chalet. Lights shimmered in the valley. The last of the day lingered in the western sky, and the Milky Way hung low overhead. It was uncannily quiet, even the breeze had fallen silent. Just us and the stars. But not one deigned to fall.

Sitting like that, heads jerked skywards, was uncomfortable, so we lay ourselves down on the broad, sturdy table. Head to head, ears touching. We talked about anything and everything. Reminisced some more about childhood. Then he told me about his girlfriend. About how much he loves her. Though she no longer does.

Later it got seriously cold, but we were loath to head back into the warmth: we still hadn't seen a single star fall over Brentschen.

Finally we headed back inside to sleep, it was really late now.

Before going to bed I popped into his room to say good night.

"You know, Dad, if I ever have a son and he asks me to recall some happy moments with my father, I'll definitely think back to tonight—to how we lay on the table under the night sky here in Brentschen, watching stars fall."

"But not a single one did."

"What difference does it make!"

We were silent for a while. Then I said, "It's late. Good night! Get some sleep! We'll talk plenty more tomorrow."

"Good night!"

And then I remembered what I'd been meaning to ask him the whole day, but kept forgetting:

"Oh yes—tell me, what doesn't fit into that saucepan that's big enough to hold everything?"

"Oh come on, Dad," he laughed, "it's simple! That would be the saucepan lid!"

The lid!

But of course! How didn't I twig at once!

Translated by Leo Shtutin

The Bell Tower of San Marco

"'Be fruitful and multiply!' Can that really be all that's bequeathed to us? Why even the mice and Koch's microbes honor this behest. But man is infinitely greater than his physical self. And how can you reduce all of me, all my untapped resources, the yearning to accomplish something important, essential, that serves mankind, my people, my country—to propagation!"

That is what Lydia Kochetkova writes in October 1898, to her future husband, Fritz Brupbacher.

I first came across this remarkable love story when I was collecting material for my *Russian Switzerland*. Six thousand letters and postcards are preserved in the archives of the International Institute of Social History in Amsterdam.

Seventeen years of a broken era are captured in this correspondence.

Brupbacher was almost unknown in Russia, and not even a footnote in Switzerland, yet against the dull background of Swiss politicians, he stood out for an 'un-Swiss' trait—his inability to compromise. A doctor in a working class district of Zurich, a deputy to the city council, a dedicated internationalist, essayist, socialist, he was expelled from the Swiss Socialist Party during World War I for his pacifism. Though a founder of the Swiss Communist Party, in 1932 he was also expelled from its ranks for excoriating Stalin. An author of socialist brochures and engaging memoirs, he had a true command of the language, and before his death in January 1945 at age 70, he regretted not having become a writer.

It's interesting that on the initiative of this very Fritz Brupbacher, a memorial plaque to Lenin was mounted on Spiegelgasse 14. Fritz knew Lenin and many other Russian revolutionaries, both sung and unsung.

As a medical student in 1897 in Zurich, Fritz met a Russian girl and fell in love. She became his wife. In his memoirs, "60 Years as a Heretic," published in 1935, he said of this union, "I was married to the Russian Revolution."

Lydia Kochetkova was 25 when she met Brupbacher. Born in Samara, she attended courses for women in Petersburg given by Lesgaft, a famous physician, then studied in Berlin, Geneva, and Berne. It was in Zurich that she took her MD and found the love of her life.

"A doctor—that's a path, not a goal," Lydia writes in an early letter, pointing out to Fritz the difference between Swiss and Russian medical students. "My goal is revolution."

Lydia's idol was Vera Figner, a physician and member of the People's Will Party, following whose example Lydia came to medical school in Switzerland. In her memoirs, Figner sheds light on the special way Russian students saw their future profession—a doctor could spread propaganda freely among the people.

The Russian air was filled with revolutionary ideals then. As for the Kochetkov family, they had their own special involvement with the revolutionaries. Though almost nothing is known of Lydia's father, who died early, her letters reveal that from childhood she was intrigued with the stories of her mother, Anastasia Ivanovna, a native of Irkutsk. She told of how, as a starry-eyed schoolgirl, the great iconoclast Prince Kropotkin, then still a tsar's officer, asked for her hand, and how her parents refused him. The young Anastasia, who was close to revolutionary circles and herself at one time under secret surveillance, was courted by two prominent members of the People's Will Party, Lazarev and Shishko. As émigrés in Switzerland, these two influenced Lydia to join its successor, the Socialist Revolutionary Party.

Even before meeting Fritz, Lydia had a clear purpose in life. "I'm ready to sacrifice everything I have for the sake of my people."

It's no small wonder this Russian woman impressed the young Helvetian. Fritz recalls, "The Russian students despised us Swiss medical students who aimed for a solid profession and a solid income. In Lydia's eyes, the Swiss, just like the other Western Europeans, had, on the whole, many failings: narrow-mindedness, a fixation on material values, opportunism, crassness and egoism. The Swiss student had his eye on dividends and a profitable marriage, the Russian on altering the world. She infected me with Socialism, had me reading certain books, took me to meetings. I was so dazzled by her and her burning faith in the socialist ideal I was ready to follow her anywhere."

A fascination with socialist thinking and the allure of all things Russian were intertwined in his feelings for Lydia. "This Russian woman was for me a complete revelation, a bundle of passion, raw emotions and rare power. Our differences showed up everywhere, everyday, in the way we spoke, and thought, in the smallest detail, even how we prepared for exams: the Swiss took this fortress over a long-month's siege, the Russians—in a head-on attack."

Many years later, when he was trying to make sense of this faith in Socialism gripping the Russian youth, Fritz writes, "For her the people and love of the people was like a religion. But you couldn't say the word 'religion' in her presence. She longed for martyrdom—to be exiled to Siberia or, better still, end up on the gallows. These young Russians were like the early Christians, marching to their execution with tears of joy."

Fritz described the 'altar' in her tiny room—engravings and photographs of revolutionary martyrs such as Countess Sophia Perovskaya, Vera Figner, and other female terrorists.

"Socialism for the Russians," we read further in his memoirs, "really meant a loss of one's ego through self-abnegation. Everything else was secondary. It was a passion to live for others. Lydia sacrificed her interest in the natural sciences to become a doctor, live among the common people, and devote herself to them. She abhorred tsarism. Her models were the regicides of the Perovskaya circle. This fervor, felt at the core, for self-sacrifice to an idea, this desire to efface her ego confused me and at the same time held something magical for one about whom the world said, 'Without money, there are no Helvetians.'"

The two were thrust together by their love despite all their emotional and cultural differences.

In her letter of 25 July, 1899 she writes, "Don't worry that I fell in love with you because you became a socialist. If Socialism were all that counted here, I would have fallen in love with some like-minded fellow like Bebel, not you. Your conversion removed any possible obstacle to our love. Ever since you became a socialist I forget you're a socialist and I love you because I love you. I'm so happy."

And in another letter of the same year, "My sweetheart! I love you precisely because you're not at all like a Swiss! I could never fall in love with one of those philistines who just think of their own little house and vegetable garden! Right away I sensed in you one of us."

Living in the same city and meeting often, they wrote each other daily, and even several times a day.

Now with a medical degree, Fritz opened a practice in Aussersihl, a working class district of Zurich, and became active politically. The workers elected him their deputy to the city council. Lydia too finished her university course and it was time to think about their life together.

He proposed marriage, but the young woman had neither the intention nor the wish to tie her fate to Switzerland. She saw herself as a doctor in the Russian backwoods. The two were in a quandary—both wanted to fight for Socialism, he in his homeland among the Zurich workers, she in Russia among the peasants. And yet both wanted to be together.

To make matters worse, Lydia's views on the family as a social institution were unconventional. "The very word marriage disgusts me," Lydia writes in November 1900. "You and I are a new kind of people, we're the future, and our relations will be the kind these philistines just don't know about. I hate their phony marriage! Everything will be different with us!"

The couple entered into a nuptial agreement that was unusual for its time: they allowed each other the freedom to choose where they wanted to live and agreed not to have children.

"Their marriages are a lie. Our marriage is a protest," she writes to her fiancé. "We're going against the current. My sweetheart, I'm proud of you! I'm proud of us! Your love is the most wonderful, the most precious thing I have."

But despite this declaration, she asserts the opposite in the very same letter. "Yet there exists something stronger and greater than love for an individual."

Her parents' marriage told on Lydia's feelings. "I know the family can destroy the self. My own mother is a great or better still, pitiful example of this. She was crushed by her marriage. A girl with ideals turned into a bourgeois, idle madam, frittering away her life at resorts. Without a higher calling. Her children grew up, went their way, and she was left with an emptiness within and without.

In Lydia's imagination the traditional family presented itself as the source of human unhappiness. "Even as a child I heard my mother say her marriage made her miserable. Though it was for love, she came to hate her husband, saw in her children the cause of her unhappiness, and felt her spark was snuffed out. She never tired of repeating that her children tied her hands and that because of them she couldn't realize her potential."

Lydia had strained relations with her mother and brother Vyacheslav. Anastasia Ivanovna lived mostly abroad on funds left by her husband. Lydia branded her a "social wastrel," although she, in turn, was supported by money her mother sent her regularly. "Sure, she's smart, energetic, and capable. But what use is this to mankind? Sure, she increased the earth's population by two, but that happened against her will. Why did she show up on this planet anyway? Was it for spa treatments?"

And again about her mother. "What terrible words I'm about to write—I find my mother despicable and more than anything in the world don't want to be like her. My poor mama! What happened to you? Why? My life won't be like yours."

Fritz recalls, "The first male she became aware of was her father, who remained fixed in her mind as a repulsive drunk. Her memories of childhood were of endless family scandals and humiliations of her mother. Lydia cut herself off from her brother Vyacheslav as well, because he didn't share her revolutionary ideals. She saw no good in her family. At bottom she was very lonely."

In a later letter, sent in December 1913, Lydia writes, "You talk about the importance of love in childhood. That's so true! I never had a loving person by my side. My mama, my brother, the nurse—they never were really close to me. I never had a true friend. All of them were surrogates, people who pretended to be close but who never really were. But I wanted to be loved so much! And no one but you was ever really interested in what was happening to me inside."

The couple often discussed their decision not to have children.

"Having children," Lydia argues, "puts an end to all my dreams of a real and productive life. Sooner or later I have to make a choice between children and the realization of my ideals. One or the other must be sacrificed. And besides, if I'm prepared to give my life, how can I leave a child in this world? Who will take care of it?"

She tried to find reasons for not having children and she succeeded: "How can we bring them into the world the way it is. We'll be ashamed to look them in the eye. First the world needs to be changed. Fritz, my love, I so want to be a mother, but I can't even consider it. I must say no to it and sacrifice a child to something far more significant."

Physical intimacy too was troublesome. She confesses her fear of the carnal. "My dear, I love you but I can't open up to you. Each time something stops me. I want to hold you close, but something keeps me back. I implore you to be patient!"

Typically, Fritz reined in his feelings, but an Amsterdam archive contains his diary with his innermost thoughts, as in the entry of 30 June, 1901. "This is insane. I can't live without her any more. Lydia's my future, my life. Without her my whole existence counts for nothing. I never knew what love was before. Being intimate is a big problem for us, but I'm ready to wait as long as it takes to help her. She's tormented. She recoils from the physical. She hates 'human flesh.' She hinted that something terrible had happened to her, perhaps when she was growing up, something connected to a man's violence. Today she said it's hard to overcome what she sees as man's animal nature, but she'll make an effort for my sake. I want this too but I'm afraid I'll turn out to be for her this very same animal. And that's exactly what I don't want!"

The discussion on physical intimacy went on for months, but they couldn't come to a decision. Over and over again she writes, "It's just instinct. We must suppress the animal in us, because we're people and not animals.

But I love you and see how you're suffering. What you want will definitely happen, just give me time, my beloved!"

The moment came when she had to decide whether to stay with Fritz or leave for Russia to fulfill her dream. She vacillates. "My sweetheart! I feel love for you in every cell of my body! Sometimes such a wave of feeling sweeps over me I could give up everything that was important to me and become your wife, give you children, look after the house, make sure your shirts are clean and ironed! But then suddenly I'll realize, as if doused with a bucket of ice water, that it's you who'll fall out of love with me first because it won't be me anymore."

The couple was officially married in the Zurich town hall and her final decision about leaving was delayed until their honeymoon. In July, 1902, they left for Italy. From Milan they went on to Venice. Fritz hoped the very atmosphere of this city of lovers would help them.

On 14 July, the day before their arrival, the Bell Tower of San Marco, the famous tower on the Piazza San Marco, symbol of Venice, collapsed. Fritz notes in his diary, "Should I take this as a sign? As a bad omen of our family life for the century to come? Maybe the 20th century really began with this catastrophe and not with a calendar date. It's amazing no one was hurt. Maybe that's a sign too! If only this century goes down as the happiest for mankind!"

They would return to this trip often in their letters.

Among Fritz's writings in the Amsterdam archive is a manuscript of an unfinished, 25 page novel, *The Bell Tower of San Marco.* The main characters, a young couple, journey to Venice, a city which should become their paradise, but where they land in the hell of a tangled relationship.

Fritz's diary entries express despair. "What terrible words—wife, husband. Newlyweds. Can this be us? It's like we're actors in some trashy play. Venice! It's the fashion for newlyweds to come here and swoon at these elegant decorations. Suddenly I'm sick of everything, most of all these masked gondoliers! This place was invented so that visitors pretend they're happy just because they came here. But the locals sell them this happiness. It's disgusting!"

The next morning he writes, "Had a terrible night. Lydia's impossible. I'm impossible. I blame only myself. We're in heaven, but we feel ourselves banished. She said she wouldn't be at breakfast. I'm sitting alone on the terrace looking at the lagoon. Some sparrows are going after something on the table. I have to keep waving them away. There's a dead pigeon on the shore. A gull's picking at its guts. Why did I expect to find happiness in Venice? With each passing day I love Lydia more and more."

Out of this trip came a resolve that each would fight for a bright future for their own people, in their own country and, as far as possible, meet every year.

In Petersburg, Lydia passed her State exam, which allowed her to practice medicine throughout the Russian empire. She was sent to the Smolensk region, in the village of Krapivnya, 45 versts from the railway station. Finally her dream of serving the people was about to come true.

But then reality quickly sobered her up.

"40 miserable hovels, cheap vodka that's government-subsidized, a church, and two peasants dead drunk in a snowdrift. There's nothing else out here. A doctor's called only for an autopsy or a recruitment exam. They doctor themselves. It's barbaric. There's no concept of hygiene, let alone order and keeping things neat and clean. Everything is swarming with parasites. Fleas, lice, roaches everywhere. You can't prescribe enemas for children or douches for women because the peasants have neither money nor the desire to buy these things. They're not even sold at the grocery or the State store that's only stocked with cheap vodka. No other stores around for a good 100 versts. No one knows about a knife and fork here, and they eat without plates—everyone just spoons out something from a pot at the same time and mothers give their children chewed food from their mouth. No wonder that fighting infections under such conditions turns into a bitter comedy. Syphilis is everywhere. Adults and children, men and women have genital warts. Trachoma is epidemic. Everyone's infecting each other. It's impossible to stop it. You can imagine how helpless I feel. Yesterday a peasant came with his son. The boy had chopped off his finger with an axe. Instead of keeping the wound clean, the father wound a spider web from the stove corner around the stump. Now I'm afraid the boy will get blood poisoning."

Well, very likely the only surprising thing for the readers of today in these letters was how the post office functioned. Letters from St. Petersburg to Zurich arrived in all of three days and from Krapivnya in less than a week.

The Zurich student who dreamed of serving her people met this people head on for the first time and was full of disappointment. Most of all she's appalled by the coarseness and cruelty of Russian life.

"You put me and my work on a pedestal, because you're so far away and can't even imagine what I'm up against every day!" she tells Fritz in the spring of 1903. "Neither civilization nor Christianity has reached these people yet. You should see how savagely they go at each other when they're drunk. How they beat up their wives and children!"

Once, in a weak moment she writes, "I remember your green lamp, your eyes, beard, your books, your pipe. I see you filling it and blowing smoke at the ceiling. If only I could be with you now. I blame myself for upsetting you instead of being affectionate when we were together."

At this time Lydia's mother was living in Lausanne, sending her money and begging her to return to Switzerland. Lydia wouldn't hear of it. "I'm having a hard time, but that's exactly why I'll stay here. To spite her!

Leaving, giving up—that's admitting defeat. I'll fight on!"

The steady flow of letters with Fritz helped her in this struggle.

In the letters, Fritz gave Lydia full support, but in his diary he was more honest with himself, revealing his doubts.

"There's theory and then there's practice. In theory, of course, I'm for sexual equality and independence of partners. I'd even sign that marriage contract of ours again. But how far we are from real life! How painful it is to live apart! I can't go on this way. It's night. At night I'm no fighter but the most ordinary fellow. I want a family, a home, a child—only I'm afraid to say it openly. Then, after a sleepless night and a moment's drifting off before dawn, morning comes. And I take myself in hand. Again I'm ready to push ahead. And my Lydia helps me. Our letters give us both strength."

A few days later there's another entry on what keeps haunting him. "By day there are my patients. They need me. Then there are meetings, speeches, the city council, time with the workers—I write an article—but in the evening, at night, I sink into a funk. I want so much to press her to me, embrace her, make love to her!"

And again he's of two minds. "Lydia and I promised each other we'd bear together the whole weight of our common cause, to renounce our petty world for the sake of a greater one, our personal life for the sake of humanity. And I will keep my word."

Their long separation took its toll. The question of faithfulness crops up.

"The only important thing is whether you love me," Lydia claims. "Because while you love me, I need you to be faithful. But if you fall out of love with me, then you're free. I won't need you to be faithful any longer."

They kept writing about how they couldn't wait to see each other and finally, in June 1903, after working a year in the backwoods of Smolensk, Lydia traveled to her husband in Switzerland. However, subsequent letters suggest they both weren't exactly ecstatic about this long awaited tryst.

En route to Zurich, she sent him a post card from Moscow. "It's so wonderful I'm on the way to see you! That's the greatest happiness I can imagine!" Departing Zurich in the fall she writes, "My darling, why are our meetings filled more with sadness than joy? I'm despicable. Just like that I can turn, without knowing why, become vulgar, rigid, even cruel, and all this towards those most close to me. I hurt them for no reason and then I regret it and cry. Forgive me, my beloved! Forgive me!"

Fritz notes in his diary, August 1903: "How can that be? To love someone from afar is one thing, but to love a real person right next to you, that's something else. It seems like we're very close in our letters, but when we meet we draw apart. Why is that? I don't understand. It pains me. We're better off in letters than in real life. Maybe that's why she didn't stay in Zurich and left for a resort in Marbach? Maybe her health was only an excuse? I'm beginning to think we're actually both afraid of our meetings. We take refuge in our letters. They're our escape from the impossibility of being either together or apart."

In the fall Lydia returned to Russia, now settling in as a local doctor in the village of Aleksandrovo, 12 versts from the town of Sudogda in Vladimir Oblast.

The impressions of the new locale and work hardly differed from what was in her letter from Krapivnya. "The outpatient department is past description—cramped, dirty, squalid. I'm here alone for 150 villages in the area. I can't sleep at night for the hordes of bloodthirsty bugs. A chicken that flew in the window broke the mirror so now I don't even know what I look like. Maybe that's for the best. They don't trust me. An old woman treats a hernia in the old way by biting people. Vodka takes care of all other ills. They pour it on wounds and sores and in the eyes for trachoma."

Fritz complained of the difficulty of getting the Swiss workers interested in Socialism, to which she replies, "Everything you say about your workers is pure Eldorado compared to what's going on here. It's hard enough for an educated person to go out among the people, but if it's the Russian people, then that requires eternal optimism. And it's especially difficult for someone who's lived so long in Europe."

Each new letter brought fresh doubts about herself and the wisdom of her choice. "I keep asking myself if I'm capable at all of practicing medicine. I sit by myself and cry my eyes out. My sole consolation is writing you about it. My beloved, if it weren't for you I couldn't go on."

In October an accident occurred for which she blamed herself and which strongly affected how the peasants saw her. "I poisoned someone. An 80 year old man got drunk and since the liquor store was already closed and you couldn't get your hands on vodka anywhere, he drank up the vial of medicine I had given him. Atropine eye drops. Tomorrow's the funeral. Now his children and the whole village hate me. They stood under my window, screaming curses and threats. Again they're all getting drunk and again at night I'll try to fall asleep and tremble from fear."

In another letter she told how a drunk was pestering her and how she had to grab an ax in self-defense. "He sobered up in a flash. But now I have to go to sleep with an ax by my bed because the lock's loose."

Again she's plagued by uncertainty. "I remember how I dreamed in Zurich of the great goal of working among the people for the people, of sacrificing myself for them. This isn't the same people they meant when they said Socialism lives in the heart of our people. So where is this Russian people. Take me to them!"

After working a year and a half in Vladimir Oblast, Lydia decided she must dedicate herself fully to the revolution.

"The more frustrated I am in what I'm doing, the more my hatred grows.

It's impossible to create anything here. It's all a waste. One must first destroy this system which keeps people from living as humans. These people are like animals because they don't know another way. Life in Russia corrupts them. You can't survive here without the basest instincts. Remember we studied this! It's natural selection. Here only the lowlife and parasites survive, the blockheads and boors. We need to alter life itself, down to the bare bones. This whole rotten system has to go. Yes, I hate this unjust world. Now my direction is clear!"

Thus, Lydia resolved to become a professional revolutionary.

"My darling," she writes in late 1904. "Once again I feel strength and confidence in myself and my future. All the hesitations and depression are in the past. I often revisit in memory our Venice and the countless times I asked myself if I acted wisely then. And now I'm happy I made the right choice. And I know, my beloved, that you'll support me."

The following year, with the onset of the Russo-Japanese War and growing mass restlessness, Lydia decided she must take her place among those leading the Russian people against tsarism. She traveled to Switzerland, home to the headquarters of all the radical parties, and on the road from Petersburg sent Fritz an ebullient letter. "There's revolution in the air at last! We, the entire Russian intelligentsia, believe and hope the Japanese will give it to the Russians. A defeat will shake the people's trust in the government. All around us is discontent and a weakening State. Great moments in history come only once in a lifetime. Glorious revolutions only once in a century. What bliss to live to see it, to prepare it, to be part of it! Long live the revolution!"

She was closest to the Socialist Revolutionary Party and spent almost all of 1905 in Geneva, renting a room in the very same building that housed their headquarters. She met Party leaders and waited impatiently to return to her homeland with an important assignment. She frequented the circle of known revolutionaries, was friends with the radicals Breshko-Breshkovskaya and Vera Figner, and also got to know Vladimir Burtsev, activist and scholar, who would expose the double agent Yevno Azef. Burtsev really impressed her and she didn't suspect the role he'd play in her fate.

She was 33. She was happy to find her life's purpose. Her letters to Zurich expressed this delight in her upcoming work and a twinge of sadness that she hadn't as yet been sent to Russia.

Finally, when the revolution was already losing steam, she traveled to Saratov, assigned to resurrect the crippled Party organization and oversee the spread of revolutionary propaganda. She was also to supervise the preparation for land expropriations and peasant revolts. The Party directives called for immediate initiation of local riots, which would boil over into a full-blown revolution. From 1906 to 1908, Lydia was the Party representative in the Saratov province.

At first her letters from this place on the Volga were optimistic. Party membership inspired her. "It's so important to feel yourself a part of something big, important, and meaningful. I'm happy as I never was before. If I pay for this for my life, that's a small price to pay for what I now feel."

The chance to be rid of one's ego, to give it up, to meld into a great communal endeavor, gave meaning to her existence. She thought she had found what she was striving for all these years. "My family is my comrades. No matter where I am, I'm part of one great family—the Party. Most likely in this sense of belonging, of kinship, I've finally discovered what I was looking for all my life."

As had Fritz, she compared this experience to a religious ecstasy. "Yes, indeed we truly resemble first century Christians—the same firm faith in the approaching, joyous salvation of the world, the same readiness to sacrifice, the same denial of the ego, of the philistine, of material things, of children, of everything that detracts from the grand idea. The difference being that religion is a lie and revolution, the truth!"

In a letter of 2 May, 1906, she described a boat trip along the Volga for an International Workers' Day picnic on an island. "We returned at night. There was a huge moon, and my darling, I suddenly remembered our Venice and that moon of ours! And what an aching sadness welled up in me. I burst into tears. My comrades began to make fun of me and we broke into revolutionary songs. I tingled from tip to toe! My beloved! We're so far from one another! And so close!"

At the end of May she reported excitedly about an assassination attempt on the Saratov prison's warden. But in her next letter she sounded pensive. The accused, a 17-year-old apprentice to a metal worker in the railroad shops where Lydia's comrades distributed proclamations, had failed. "Shatalov, the warden, recovered and got promoted and went to work for Prime Minister Stolypin. The prison has a new warden. They hung the boy. So now I can't stop thinking—is this why that child was born and lived out his 17 years? He's truly a hero and won't be forgotten by progressive Russia. One day they'll erect a monument to him, but I can't bear to think of his last moments before the gallows. And what if he repented of his act? How terrible it was then for him to die!"

Still, in the following letter, Lydia cast off all her doubts. Her conscience troubled her for being a crybaby and that her faith was shaken. Once again she threw herself into revolutionary work. In the summer of 1906, she was sent by the Party to spread propaganda in the Atkarsk district of Saratov province. She was able to regulate the publication and distribution of leaflets and then became involved in the delivery of weapons and the organization of expropriations.

On 1 October, 1906, Lydia, euphoric, writes to Zurich from Atkarsk about the destruction of landed estates. "Expropriations going on throughout the whole province! Our people are the most marvelous on earth! Its soul is as close to Kropotkin's anarchism as they come. Total disregard for the law, no understanding whatsoever of this word. The expropriations proceed so simply, with the effortlessness of those who have no compunctions when it comes to property, theirs and others, only communist instincts."

But soon after, her disenchantment deepened. By the minute she awaited the start of a universal revolution. Her task was to organize militant peasant divisions and stir up revolts, but not only didn't the revolution take hold, on the contrary, it burned out. Prime Minister Stolypin instilled order with his ruthless measures and formulated reforms. Because of the work of double agents, they arrested revolutionaries en masse.

"The snow's gone," she writes in March 1907, "but instead of revolts, they're sowing. And my heart tells me that this year there won't be any revolution! Our program—a call for local uprisings—that's one thing. But it seems peasant life is another story. The moment the sowing or harvest of the crop begins, the peasant loses all revolutionary zeal. Everyone, young and old, is out in the fields. All they really care about is daily survival, the here and now, not the visionary socialist republic of tomorrow."

She began to reflect on Russian women, simple peasants, whom it was necessary to awaken to the struggle against tsarism. "I compare myself with these peasant women. They have no time to think about saving mankind, no time to worry about the people's happiness. They have to save their own family, their children, to think about how to feed them. I want to invest all of me into trying to free them, but a doubt creeps in—what if they don't need any part of me altogether? What sad thoughts come to me in these sleepless nights."

In one of her next letters she talks about how the peasants confuse expropriation with looting. "They take away everything bit by bit to their homes, and the estates look like barbarians had been there. I was on such an estate—everything plundered, the pierced eyes in portraits, piles of excrement everywhere, in the most conceivable and inconceivable places. My God, how come there's so much excrement coming from my people? I see our revolution completely differently."

More and more she's repelled by the brutality of events. In October of that year she writes, "They slaughtered the landowner's entire family—two kids, a boy and a girl. Not even the doctor who was with them was spared, nor the French governess, who, by the way, came from Switzerland. I try to tell myself that that's the way it must be, that without blood and violence there are no great revolutions. But the whole point is that I must keep convincing myself. It's so hard for me, my beloved! People carry such hatred! And now a firing squad has come from Saratov, killing peasants from the neighboring village, not really caring who's guilty and who isn't. And all around the hatred is growing. And again I need to tell myself we're living in the most wonderful, uplifting times, and that this violence will be the last."

Her apprehension about the expropriations intensified. "If this violence floods the whole country, it will be hard to stop it. For that you need even more violence. It's horrible!"

Lydia traveled several times to Europe during her three year stay in Saratov province. In 1908, for instance, under the pseudonym Volgina, she cast the deciding vote from the Saratov organization in the Party conference in London, even making a speech there. Each time she made a trip to Switzerland and reunited with her husband, but their meetings were becoming all too brief.

In Fritz's diary of 1908 we read of Lydia's visit to Zurich. "We're growing further and further apart. Again I told her I want to finally be together, that I'm prepared to work in Russia and even study Russian.

After all, the great Swiss doctor Friedrich Erismann went off to claim his wife in Moscow and started a clinic there. I'm not the first or the last. We talked again about a child. The kind of marriage we have can't go on. Her reaction: "'Family happiness is not for revolutionaries.'"

The ultimate unmasking of the double agent Azef not only reverberated throughout the whole Socialist Revolutionary Party, but shook Lydia's seemingly indestructible faith in the cause of the revolution itself. Party activity practically stopped. Former comrades began to suspect each other of provocation. For Lydia, working in such circumstances became impossible and futile.

"You can't do something if you don't believe you'll succeed," she writes in 1909 from Atkarsk to Zurich. "The Party's falling apart. Party work has stalled. Its very heart has been pierced—everyone sees only provocation in everything, no one believes anyone. What am I doing here? There are no cultured people in Atkarsk, just philistines, and you can't really call them people. You can only find the proletariat in the big cities. Here it's all darkness, boredom, poverty, drunkenness, right wing nationalists, filth, in a nutshell, the Russian province, which it seems you have to either blow up or escape. It's impossible to live here. I feel old, look terrible, my hair's getting grey. I'm wrinkled. Life's passing me by. In three years of daily labor I've not brought my dream of my country's and my people's great future even a jot closer, not matter how I've tried. Among my comrades there's constant squabbling, mutual distrust and hatred. They hate their own more than they do strangers. I have to be an arbiter in their tedious Party trials. And I'm horrified that my love for this family, which I believed I finally found, is disappearing. I can't believe these embittered, useless people are my family."

She lost faith not only in her Party comrades but in the peasants. "It all boils down to the fact that they don't need any revolution. What they're after is the good life, dull but comfortable. To fire them up for revolution you don't need drunken pillages, but a war. And not with Japan, but something real and big that rocks the government to its very foundations, so that trouble and hatred comes to each home, so that each peasant gets a rifle. Only then can the revolution blow up Russia. But will there be that revolution of which we dreamed, which we prepared, for whose sake we sacrificed ourselves and everyone around?"

Lydia sank into a deep depression.

"I'm still stuck here, waiting for something, but my escape from this hateful town, where nothing happens and will never happen, is long overdue. I'm like Firs who's left behind in Chekhov's *The Cherry Orchard*—everyone's gone, but they forgot me."

She tried again to go on with her medical practice, but couldn't. "I have no medical books here, and not enough experience. I didn't turn out a revolutionary or a doctor. I'm left with nothing."

Profoundly distraught, she traveled again to Switzerland in early 1909. "Maybe, it's not at all about the people's happiness or revolution, maybe, I simply wanted to be happy in the one life given me and was ready to sacrifice myself for the sake of personal happiness? So then, how can we call it a 'sacrifice'? Sometimes it seems I got all knotted up in myself, in my life—in everything. Fritz, my beloved, I'm in a bad way. Really bad. I mean emotionally. As for my body, it doesn't matter to me anymore."

Lydia Kochetkova went for the last time to Switzerland for treatment and again stayed at the Marbach sanatorium on Lake Boden. But the stay was brief. Flight from herself became a way of life. She couldn't explain to Fritz her decision to return to Russia. Nor, it seems, to herself. After visiting his wife in the sanatorium, Fritz writes, "Lydia can't possibly get back to herself after all that's happened in the last years. She looks terrible."

In any event, on 1 July, 1909, Lydia Petrovna Kochetkova crossed the border of the Russian empire and was arrested on the spot.

Following a brief imprisonment, she was exiled for three years to Arkhangelsk province, initially to the village of Ustvashka. In her first letters from there one can still detect a note of pride. For the Russian intellectuals, arrest, hard labor or exile traditionally served as a kind of Communion. But all too soon her tone changed.

"I have much time now to reflect on my life," she writes in September, 1909, from Ustvashka. "Here it's the same as all over Russia—dirt, backwardness, drunkenness, violence. The other day a neighbor stabbed his wife. Each year, in every village, someone gets killed. We worshiped the people, but they're werewolves. Why love them? And the exiles are contentious, hostile, and hate each other. There's not a drop of faith left in me, least of all in the revolution. Actually I feel only dread. What if the revolution really happened? We made the mess and it's for our children and grandchildren to clean it up. Sometimes I think it's just as well I have no child. You see, I'm not in a very good mood. My letters to you are all I can hold on to. I'm drowning."

In the winter she was transferred to Pinega, where she contracted typhus. Fritz rushed off to her in this remote exile. He traveled through Moscow and Petersburg to Arkhangelsk, and from there six more days by sled.

And again, as so often before, their time together brought no joy. When he left she wrote, "Why do we love each other more when we're apart? Tell me!"

We know from Fritz' diary that for him this visit was a turning point in his relationship to his wife.

On route to Moscow he makes this entry: "I no longer have any illusions. We do not have and cannot have any real closeness—letters are one thing—but life's something completely different. We're close only with thousands of kilometers between us. Probably Lydia's a certain kind of woman—a woman wired for self destruction and not the continuation of life. All her life she's been destroying herself and dragging down everyone around her. Once she and I read Russian novels about superfluous people. She's one of them. I can't bear it. I'm a part of life and life's a part of me. I must give her up. I've never felt such bitterness and such pain."

Then and there he sent a letter from Moscow telling her he wanted to break off the relationship. "Lydia, I'm beside myself. I have to let you go and follow my own path. I'm healthy, not old yet. I want a nest, comfort, a family. At night I want to come home. We'll never have this together. We have to let each other go."

Fritz asked for a divorce. She agreed but kept writing to him because these letters were the last thing left to her. This blow coincided with another blow of fate from which she was unable to recover.

It came out in Pinega that Burstev, whom Lydia had greatly admired, circulated a letter abroad accusing her of being a provocateur and working for the tsarist secret police.

"I can only think of how vile people are," she tells Fritz in despair. "I would have born everything from my enemies. But to be knocked down by my own kind? I thought I had found a family among my comrades, but instead I found treachery and slander. My whole life is destroyed, everything I held sacred—sullied and debased. As if my very soul were trampled and smeared. I can't go on. I don't want to. I've nothing left to believe in. I do not want to and cannot go on."

Lydia begged her former husband to contact Burtsev in Paris and clear up this monstrous misunderstanding. Fritz wrote to him, but it's not known if Burstev ever answered.

She felt cornered. "People shun me like a leper. All the exiles turn away from me. Around me there's only contempt and hatred. How can one live when everyone hates you? But maybe this hatred is a punishment for the hatred I felt for my enemies. So now I'm for my comrades the enemy. What should I do? Should I forgive everyone everything? No, I can't do that. Anyhow, I have no strength left for forgiveness or hate. Should I hang myself? But that won't prove my innocence."

She resolved to break for good with the Socialist Revolutionary Party, which had been her faith and truth.

After exile there was no place for her to go. She had no home. No one was waiting for her anywhere. In 1911 she arrived in Moscow from Pinega and stayed at her estranged brother Vyacheslav's, with whom she had once broken all ties. Her mother was living there too.

Lydia continued sending anguished letters to Zurich.

With each letter she seemed to be closing the door on her life.

"Life passes and I still don't know why I came into this world. I gave nothing to anyone. I'm worthless. I lost faith in myself. I don't belong among people. Not even the closest ones. I start the day trading curses with my mother. And my brother. And his wife. With my mother it hurts the most. There's no bridge between us, not even the tiniest sliver. Loneliness. Old age. I'm 40, but I look 60. She's 60 and looks every bit 80. How awful when it suddenly hits you that at least she has me and Vyacheslav, distant and alien, but still her own children. But what and whom do I have? No one. And there'll be no one any more. My one wish is to crawl away as far as possible from people and quietly croak."

In another letter, sent in the fall of 1913, she tried to make sense of her past, to sort out important moments in her life, and again reminded him of Venice. "My love, I cannot describe to you the state I'm in. I'm the most wretched person on earth. I never thought that one could be that wretched. The only thing I had was you, our love, that gift which I received and spurned. Then, in Venice it was all still possible. I committed an error.

Everything I chose over life with my beloved turned out a lie. Everything is a lie. Lofty ideas are a lie. The revolution is a lie. The people are a lie. All the beautiful words are a lie, a lie, a lie. Yet I blame no one. Only I am responsible for my wasted life. Then, in Venice, it was still possible to change everything. Or was it already impossible? I don't know. I don't know anything more. I no longer exist. The sooner I die, the better. My body still drags around from inertia, but the soul's gone. It's long dead. Do you know what my ideal is now? To disappear quietly, unnoticed, so that I leave nothing, not even my corpse."

She continued writing to him for some time, but he rarely answered. Most likely these letters are all that is left of her.

Their correspondence broke off during the First World War.

Nothing is known of Lydia Petrovna Kochetkova's death.

This is from the last available letter.

"My darling! Do you know what I regret most of all? I could have given you all the fullness of my love, but I gave you nothing but pain. Forgive me, if you can. And my heart cries out at the thought that my highest calling was just that—to give you my affection and tenderness, but instead I squandered my worthless life on phantoms."

Translated by Sylvia Maizell

In a Boat Scratched on a Wall

Language, as it creates reality, judges: it punishes and pardons. Language is its own verdict. There is nowhere to appeal. All higher courts are nonverbal. Even before writing anything, the writer, like Laocoön, has been pinioned by the language snake. If he is to explain anything, the writer must be freed from language.

It took quite a while after my move from Pushka to the canton of Zurich for the bizarre sensation of irreality, the carnival quality of what was happening to me, to be replaced, little by little, by the tentative and amazed confidence that, indeed, there was no deception here. The trains were not toy trains, the landscape not painted, the people not planted there.

Immediately following the change of scenery, I tried to finish writing the novel I'd begun in Moscow, but I got nowhere. The letters I'd traced out there had a totally different density here. The novel ended up being about something else. Every word is a high step you trip over.

Borders, distance, and air do wonders for words. A combination of Russian sounds that was so obvious and natural on Malaya Dmitrovka, with the Chekhov Casino raging outside, can't get through customs here. Words stripped of any independent existence there seem to take up residency here and become not a means but a subject of verbal law. Here, any Russian word sounds all wrong and means something completely different.

There, in the theater, the meaning of any spoken phrase changes with the sets.

On the banks of the Limmat, it's as if there's a different center of gravity, and any word out of a Russian inkwell weighs much more than in Russian's country of origin. What in Russia suffuses, litters the atmosphere, the sediments and snouts, Grushnitsky the cadet, the war in Chechnya, and "Christ has risen from the dead," here is all concentrated in every word written in Cyrillic—crammed, rammed into every last ы.

With each passing day, as it slips from reality, the fatherland seeks out new bearers and finds them in the squiggles of an exotic alphabet. Russia has gathered all its goods and chattel and taken up residence in a font. Letters have been consolidated just as apartments once were to accommodate new residents.

My departure from the language, my loss of Russian murmuring in my ears, forced me to stop, to be silent. On the rare occasions we meet, writers from Russia are amazed. "How can you write in this boring Switzerland? Without the language, without the tension?"

They're right. Russian letters do have high pressure. And the language there is changing quickly.

My departure from Russian speech forced me to turn around and face it. Work on my text came to a halt. Just as the pause is a part of music, so silence is a part of the text. The most important part, maybe.

What language did I leave behind? What did I take with me? Where can words go from here? The work of silence.

If I was to go further, I had to understand where the essence of writing in Russian actually lay.

Being at once creator and creature of the nation's reality, the Russian language is the form of existence, the body, of the totalitarian consciousness.

Daily life has always muddled through without words: with bellowing, interjections, jokes, and quotes from film comedies. It's the state and literature that require coherent words.

Russian literature is not the language's form of existence but the non-totalitarian consciousness's form of existence in Russia. The totalitarian consciousness is amply served by decrees and prayers. Decrees from above, prayers from below. The latter are usually more original than the former. Swearing is the vital prayer of a prison country.

Edicts and cursing are the nation's yin and yang, rain and field, phallus and vagina; they conceive Russian civilization verbally.

Over the generations, the prison reality developed a prison consciousness whose main principle was "the strongest get the best bunks." This consciousness was expressed in a language called up to serve Russian life, maintaining it in a state of continuous, unending civil war. When everyone lives by prison camp laws, language's mission is everyone's cold war with everyone else. If the strong must inevitably beat the feeble, the language's mission is to do this verbally. Humiliate him, insult him, and steal his ration. Language as a form of disrespect for the individual.

Russian reality developed a language of unbridled power and abasement. The language of the Kremlin and the prison camp slang of the street share one and the same nature. In a country that lives by an unwritten but distinct law—the weakest's place is by the slop bucket—the dialect suits the reality. Words rape. Words abuse.

Had the borders been under lock and key, there wouldn't be any Russian literature.

Literary language arrived in the eighteenth century along with the idea of human dignity. We had no words for that language. The first century of the nation's literature was essentially translations and imitations. We had no verbal instrument to express the individual consciousness. It first had to be created. Russian was taught like a foreign language, and the missing concepts were introduced: "the public," "being in love," "being humane," "literature."

The Russian literary language, which in Russia is human dignity's form of existence, its body, squeezed through the crack between the shout and the moan. Russian literature wedged into an alien embrace. It used words to construct the great Russian wall between the state and the people.

It was a foreign body, a colony of European culture on the Russian plain, if by European colonization we mean the mitigation of mores and the defense of the rights of the weak before the mighty and not the importation of German gunners.

As has happened on other continents as well, the colony outstripped the mother country in its development. Turgenev, Tolstoy, Dostoevsky—these are all colonists whose texts moved literature's capital from the Old World to Russia. They took all the best from the thousand-year legacy and said, Go east!

But something is rotten in the Russian realm, and periodically, the state and the people make a rush toward each other, and then foreigners need to watch out. Writers' bones crack in these embraces as well; they either die or slip away.

The twentieth century saw certain well-known events. The indigenous population returned once again to its usual "literary process:" decrees from above, prayers from below. Some "colonists" returned to their spiritual homeland; those who stayed had their tongues ripped out by the barbarians.

The invented language of the Soviet utopia was also the body of its existence. Socialism's lifeless, invented reality existed only in the suitably dead language of the newspapers, television, and political meetings. In the 1990s, when the regime disappeared along with the language that served it, prison camp slang rose to the top and filled the vacuum.

Once again, the state and the nation are speaking the same dialect and whacking Chechens in the toilet, as Putin so famously put it.

Today the totalitarian consciousness lives on in the language of television, where the main principle of dialog is to outshout the other guy. It is the language of newspapers turned sickeningly yellow. It is the language of the street, where swearing is the norm.

The language of Russian literature is an ark. A rescue attempt. A hedgehog defense. An island of words where human dignity is supposed to be preserved.

When I left Russia, I lost the language I wanted to lose. The changes in modern Russian are a molting. The fur seems different, but the colouration is the same, and painfully recognizable at that. This language, which is meant to debase, reproduces itself with each generation of Russian boys and girls. In and of itself, the literary language does not exist; it has to be created anew each time, and in solitude.

Finding myself in Switzerland, I first had to understand who and where I was. For me, understanding something means writing a book about it. The result was *Russian Switzerland*. Through this book, through Switzerland, I tried to understand something about myself and my country of origin.

I wanted to read this book, not write it. Strange though it may seem, the book arose out of the very fact of its absence, born from my sense of the tremendous number of holes in the Swiss landscape. There were the mountains and banks, but something more substantive was lacking. A foreign country remains foreign until you find people near and dear to you there.

I began searching for Gogol and Bunin the way a poor provincial seeks out rich relatives in the big city. I simply collected, crumb by crumb, what there was here of Tolstoy, and Scriabin, and the terrorists, and the men who fled here from Germany as Russian prisoners of war. And I ended up with the history of my country, my Russia, a country not on any map. In this country of mine, my dead parents settled between the lines, as did all my nameless Tambov ancestors, who hacked and were hacked, executed and were executed. I simply wanted to compile a "literary and historical guidebook," but it ended up being a novel about the Russian world, except that, unlike a traditional novel, uninvented characters in it live uninvented lives, or rather, lives not invented by me.

The book contains little of the real Switzerland. Switzerland is instead a strange entity by that name that exists within the Russian cultural consciousness.

Of all the Wests invented in Russia, the most invented is Karamzin's paradise West, which was invented in the eighteenth century by German and French teachers on Russian estates, surrounded by slaves. And Karamzin, a conscientious pupil, made Switzerland the symbol of that West. In his Swiss letters, which he wrote in Russia, he falls down on his knees on the banks of the Rhine outside Basel and exclaims, "Happy Swiss! Do you—every day, every hour—do you thank the heavens for your happiness, for the fact that you live in the embrace of a most splendid nature, under the beneficent laws of a most brotherly union, in the simplicity of your customs and serving one God?"

This "enlightened" version of the West was invented from its opposite. If Russia lives by the principle, "If you're the boss, I'm the fool; if I'm the boss, you're the fool," then there they have a republic, equality, elections, and so on. If in the fatherland, "righteous labor does not build man a house of stone," then there righteous labor does lead to a house of one's own "with a stork on the roof," Dostoevsky's famous expression, in *The Gambler,* for Europe's narrow burgher mentality. If in our homeland something belongs to you only until someone stronger decides to take it away, then there private property is sacred, and a peasant can be confident that his lawn will belong to his descendants ten generations hence, and so forth.

It became a book about the protracted struggle among Russian ideas, the unending national showdown, the barricades that never come down on the streets of the notorious Russian soul.

When the question arose of translating *Russian Switzerland* into German, I suddenly discovered that this book truly exists only along with my Russian reader. Any sentence spoken in Russian places you on one side of the barricades or the other. And in translation, it's not just that the associations and allusions disappear—half the names require notes—you can't even tell where the barricades are. You can translate the words, but not the reader.

Not only can no novel really be translated, neither can any word. The experience of a language and the life lived through it and any specific word make languages with different pasts noncommunicating vessels. A past alive in words defies translation, especially that Russian past which was never a fact but always an argument in the neverending war the nation has waged with itself.

If you are to build your own Russian literary ark, you have to become a hermit. Go somewhere. Anywhere—to the Alps or inward. And take along only your lived experience of love and loss and ten centuries of Cyrillic.

To know which way words are going, you need two points through which you can draw the line of motion. One point is everything written before you in Russian, beginning with the Slavonic translation of the Scriptures.

The second point is you yourself, lock, stock, and barrel, and all the people you love.

If you are going to say something new, you need to feel the centuries of tradition inside you. If a button is pushed at some power plant, the light flickers in the city's windows. So, too, in literature, if a word is written, it reverberates in all the existing books, regardless of whether you've read them or not.

Literary tradition is a living being. A plant.

Sap runs through the trunk to the branches. The nineteenth century is the trunk of Russian literature. Then comes the branching. There are perfectly brilliant branches, like Platonov, but this is a severed limb that cannot keep growing. You have to find the branch that reaches up, the main branch along which the tree grows skyward.

Chekhov. Bunin. Nabokov. Sasha Sokolov.

In my texts I mean to connect Western literature and its achievements in verbal technique with the humanity of the Russian pen. Joyce doesn't love his heroes, but Russian writers do. The Russian hero is Akaky Akakievich, from Gogol's "Overcoat." Though there is no good reason to love him.

To know which way to go, you need to turn around and see where you're coming from. What is genuinely new is always a development of the tradition. In order to understand the tradition, you need to discover the word's genetic code, seek out the living DNA spiral along which you can trace where all this came from. And if you do untwist that spiral, you will arrive at He Who loves and waits for us all. You simply need to put the words in the one and only orader (which is unknown) that makes the chain of words lock on God, so that life can run down it. The writer must find the precise order that makes real blood course under the skin of the words.

Words are the material for the road. The longest and most important road. The road to the "historical homeland"—to the ultimate beginning. "In the beginning there was love. This cluster of love. Or rather, not even love yet, but the need for it, because there wasn't anyone to love. God was lonely and cold. And this love here demanded an outlet, an object, it wanted warmth, to hold someone dear close, to sniff the delicious nape of a child, its own, flesh of its flesh, so God created himself a child to love. Nineveh" (*Maidenhair*). A novel is an opportunity to find the road to that original love. For his heroes, the author is God. The reader identifies with the hero. If the author loves his Akaky Akakievich, whom there is no good reason to love, then the reader, too, feels, knows, that God exists and loves him, though there is no good reason to. He just does. As he would his own child. This is what words are for, to pave the road to that feeling.

In time, though, any road wears out and forms ruts and potholes. Language gets played out. The road the generations have gone down becomes impassable. It grows up in clichés. You have to lay a new one. "One more novel" is written in a worn language that leads nowhere. In order to reach your goal, you need a new road, a new way of putting words together.

For me, the only way to create my own language is to write incorrectly. I sniff each sentence, and if I get a whiff of a textbook on "How To Speak and Write Correctly," I cross it out. Saying something correctly means saying nothing. Because ever since the Tower of Babel, language has been a means of misunderstanding. Correct words, having given up the ghost, can mean anything at all except what you want to say, and they evoke a sense of disdain, like someone else's scruffy toothbrush or a woman who has been passed around.

In the beginning there was love, not the word. The child has yet to be conceived, but the mother already loves him. And then, body inside body, love doesn't need words. After the birth, mother and child still love each other nonverbally. Only with words, when verbal barriers arise between people who love each other, does alienation begin.

Thus, language creates barriers. Once they lost their sacral nature, words turned into a means of misunderstanding. Words don't mean anything anymore. So you have to do something with these words to restore their original, Divine meaning.

Words are guards that keep out emotion and meaning, sentries at the boundary between people. Either you need to learn to grope your way toward understanding each other, or else be able to escape over the verbal barbed wire.

There is no road to understanding except through words.

Word corpses watch over us. The only way to get past them is to revive them. We have to breathe new life into them, so that love can once again be called love.

Each new generation of living prose is just another path leading to where each of us is loved and awaited. Tradition consists in finding language of a new clarity and writing a classic Russian novel today, a novel about love, about how God will always have compassion for Nineveh, about overcoming death, which is a boundary between people.

The Taking of Izmail is a novel about grabbing life, about overcoming death with a "collection of words" and the birth of a child. The novel's world is constructed from the elementary particles of biographies that are more substantive than fictitious. Sentence fragments are jumbled up because the mumbling coming from the anteroom of Judgment Day cannot be coherent. There, there are no longer any "intact" physical bodies, but there is still pain, joy, fear, and love, in short, the sensation of life. The person is gone, but his breath is preserved. I collect human breath.

Language has a grammatical past and future but no past or future.

In the dimension of words, time twists like a screw with a stripped thread. Time can be opened at any line. Open the first line a hundred times, and you will force Him to create heaven and earth a hundred times and race over the water. He is racing right now.

The Izmail meridian passes through Russian letters and through my life. The book begins in Russian literature and ends with the birth of my son in the Winterthur canton hospital. In Switzerland, I cut my child's umbilicus and my novel's.

The words' time, multiplied by the words' dimension, equals the style. The generally accepted unit of the novel is the character. In *Izmail,* style is a character. The scratching of styles that play the part traditionally allocated to conflicts between good and evil—between the hero's will and fate, between a man's fist and the bronze horseman, and so on—are the text's load-bearing construction. The styles are heroes that each defend their own picture of the world. It's not the edges of phrases that wrangle but the edges of worldviews.

The Taking of Izmail is a declaration of love to a monstrous fatherland. For this reason the novel turned out to be too tightly sealed, too Russian.

The Taking of Izmail is a metaphor for capturing that Russian life the way you would capture an enemy fortress.

But leaving helps you understand that King Herod, who killed children, is a matter of time and not geography at all.

That meant I had to write another novel. I had to talk about these things, and in such a way that what was written was clear to Hellene and Jew. Five years were spent on *Maidenhair.*

After arriving in "boring" Switzerland, where there was seemingly nothing to write about, I plunged into Russia. For the last few years I worked as an interpreter in the immigration service, interpreting interviews with refugees from our former fraternal republics. I translated words into destiny. No one tells unhorrific stories there. The novel's hero, "an interpreter in the refugee chancellery of the Defense Ministry of Paradise," turned out to be an interpreter between two worlds. An interface between two incompatible systems.

The Swiss bureaucrat, Peter Fischer, doesn't believe the stories he is told, and the heavenly gates remain under lock and key forever.

What really happened, no one will ever find out. But the stories told, the words, create their own reality. The details are important. Words create realities and decide destinies.

Unidentified writers, under four evangelical pseudonyms, wrote a book that made the world what it is today. Their words created the very reality in which we have been living for two thousand years; the words simply had to be worthy of faith. Had it not been for the detail about the baked fish he ate after going hungry after he died on the cross, and the finger stuck into the wound, the world would not be Christian and would not be awaiting resurrection. The word becomes the reality, a reality of which we ourselves are merely a part.

A person writing is a link between two worlds: the unreal world of life, where everything is transient, fleeting, and mortal and vanishes without a trace, like the second—or the thousands of generations—that just flashed by; and the world of words worthy of faith, which sprinkle the elixir of immortality on that baked fish, and that honey, and that finger. And on that living man whose feet both Marias rushed to embrace, death notwithstanding.

Unless life is transformed into words, there will be nothing.

The author becomes a translator translating all these people into words. In the book, refugees to Switzerland from the countries of the former Soviet Union become a metaphor for people, living and dead, trying to make their way to their own historical homeland, which is the same for all of us: God. It is the place where someone loves us all. Even if there is no good reason to love us. The author is these people's translator.

But just as Peter Fischer, Peter the Fisherman holding the keys to heaven, stands on a real border, so too language stands on the border of reality. Language itself is the world that will remain. And the border of the world beyond which you cannot poke your head. Just try. And you'll smash into language, like a window.

The author is the interface between earth and sky. Between life and text. It is he who can lead people out of time and into forever.

On the one hand, there is the fleeting, transient world where you cannot live and from which everyone flees, not because there's not enough money somewhere, not because someone is in pain there, or someone is humiliated, and not because someone was put in prison, rather everyone flees from a world when there is death in it. After taking in this world, the author at the other end must counter with something equivalent in force. For this, he must create a world without death.

Language is a means of resurrection. My novel is about there being no death. Everyone knows there is no death, but each person has to find his own proofs. And so I search. One apocrypha says, "For by the word was the world created, and by the word shall we be resurrected."

Words must be made living not only until the cock crows but so that they cannot die anymore. I have to suck dead time out of the word and blow living time in, mouth to mouth—and force it to breathe, like a drowning victim. I have to resurrect it to eternal life with our breath. I have to use words to create a reality where there is no death.

Death can be overcome only by the word and by love. This is a novel about love, which is the force of life. Maidenhair is a plant, *adiantum capillus-veneris*; in the South, in Rome, in the Eternal City, where all the lines of the novel tie up, it is a weed, but in Russia, it would perish without human love and warmth. In the novel, maidenhair is the God of life, which grew before the fleeting eternal city and will grow after it.

There is a legend about a prisoner sentenced to solitary confinement for life. He spent years scratching a boat on the wall with the handle of a prison spoon. One day, they brought him his water, bread, and gruel, as usual, but the cell was empty, and the wall was blank. He had climbed into his scratched boat and floated away.

The novel is a boat. Words have to be revived so the boat can be genuine. So it can be climbed into and float out of this lonely life and go where we are all loved and awaited. Saved. Taking me us all my heroes. And the reader.

Translated by Marian Schwartz

MIKHAIL PAVLOVICH SHISHKIN is one of the most acclaimed contemporary Russian literary figures, and the only author to win all three major Russian literary prizes (the Russian Booker Prize; the National Bestseller Prize; and the Big Book Award). Born in Moscow in 1961, Shishkin studied English and German at Moscow State Pedagogical Institute. After graduation he worked as a street sweeper, road worker, journalist, schoolteacher, and translator. He debuted as a writer in 1993, when his short story "Calligraphy Lesson" was published in *Znamya* magazine, which went on to win him the Debut Prize. Since then his works—both fiction and non-fiction—have been translated into 29 languages and have received a large number of prestigious national and international awards across the world. His prose is universally praised for its style, and his novels and stories deal with universal themes like death, resurrection, and love. Shishkin's prose fuses the best of the Russian and European literary traditions: the richness and sophistication of the language, the unique rhythm and melody of a phrase, the endless play with words and the nuanced psychological undercurrent are reminiscent of Nabokov and Chekhov. The change of narration styles and narrators within a text yield a fragmented, mosaic structure of composition that focuses on the language itself, recalling James Joyce's genius. Shishkin carries on the tradition of the greatest Russian writers, and admits to their influence in his work, "Bunin taught me not to compromise, and to go on believing in myself. Chekhov passed on his sense of humanity—that there can't be any wholly negative characters in your text. And from Tolstoy I learned not to be afraid of being naïve." Shishkin has lived mostly outside of Russia since 1994, and today lives between Germany and Switzerland.

· MARIAN SCHWARTZ began her career in literary translation in 1978, and in the three decades since then she has published over sixty volumes of fiction and nonfiction—biography, criticism, fine arts, and history. Schwartz studied Russian at Harvard University, Middlebury Russian School, and Leningrad State University and received a Master of Arts in Slavic Languages and Literatures from the University of Texas at Austin in 1975. Schwartz is perhaps best known for her prize-winning translations of works by Russian émigré writer Nina Berberova, Edvard Radzinsky's the bestseller, *The Last Tsar: The Life and Death of Nicholas II*, several novels by Andrei Gelasimov, and Mikhail Shishkin's first novel to appear in English, *Maidenhair* (Open Letter 2012). She lives in Austin, Texas.

· LEO SHTUTIN studied French literature at the University of Oxford, completing his DPhil in 2014. He translates for The Calvert Journal and other online publications. His translation from the Russian of Victor Beilis' novel *Death of a Prototype* (2005) is due to be published by Thames River Press, and a version of his DPhil thesis—an investigation of the notions of spatiality and subjectivity in the writings of Stéphane Mallarmé, Guillaume Apollinaire, Maurice Maeterlinck and Alfred Jarry—is currently being readied for publication by OUP.

· MARIYA BASHKATOVA is an alumna of Brown University, where she studied Comparative Literature and Cognitive Neuroscience. At Brown, she wrote for the school newspaper and was involved in the Aldus Journal of Translation. An avid reader, Bashkatova translates Russian and French literature.

· SYLVIA MAIZELL studied Russian Literature at the University of Chicago, in Moscow and in Saint Petersburg, and taught Russian for many years. For the last decade she worked as a translator from Russian, including stories by Vladimir Makanin, Andrei Gelasimov, Ludmila Petrushevskaya, and Dina Rubina. Her translations have appeared in *The Kenyon Review*, *Best European Fiction 2011*, *Moscow Noir*, *Russian Love Stories* (Middlebury Studies), *Metamorphoses*, *Partisan Review*, and *Dance Chronicle: Studies in Dance and Related Arts.*

Thank you all
for your support.
We do this
for you, and
could not do it
without you.

DEAR READERS,

Deep Vellum is a not-for-profit publishing house founded in 2013 with the threefold mission to publish international literature in English translation; to foster the art and craft of translation; and to build a more vibrant book culture in Dallas and beyond. We seek out works of literature that might otherwise never be published by larger publishing houses, works of lasting cultural value, and works that expand our understanding of what literature is and what it can do.

Operating as a nonprofit means that we rely on the generosity of donors, cultural organizations, and foundations to provide the basis of our operational budget. Deep Vellum has two donor levels, the LIGA DE ORO and the LIGA DEL SIGLO. Members at both levels provide generous donations that allow us to pursue an ambitious growth strategy to connect readers with the best works of literature and increase our understanding of the world. Members of the LIGA DE ORO and the LIGA DEL SIGLO receive customized benefits for their donations, including free books, invitations to special events, and named recognition in each book.

We also rely on subscriptions from readers like you to provide an invaluable ongoing investment in Deep Vellum that demonstrates a commitment to our editorial vision and mission. Subscribers are the bedrock of our support as we grow the readership for these amazing works of literature. The more subscribers we have, the more we can demonstrate to potential donors and bookstores alike the diverse support we receive and how we use it to grow our mission in ever-new, ever-innovative ways.

If you would like to get involved with Deep Vellum as a donor, subscriber, or volunteer, please contact us at deepvellum.org. We would love to hear from you.

Thank you all,

Will Evans, Publisher

LIGA DE ORO

($5,000+)

Anonymous (2)

LIGA DEL SIGLO

($1,000+)

Allred Capital Management

Ben Fountain

Judy Pollock

Loretta Siciliano

Lori Feathers

Mary Ann Thompson-Frenk & Joshua Frenk

Matthew Rittmayer

Meriwether Evans

Nick Storch

Stephen Bullock

DONORS

Alan Shockley
Amrit Dhir
Anonymous
Andrew Yorke
Bob & Katherine Penn
Brandon Childress
Brandon Kennedy
Charles Dee Mitchell
Charley Mitcherson
Cheryl Thompson
Christie Tull
Ed Nawotka
Greg McConeghy
JJ Italiano
Kay Cattarulla
Kelly Falconer
Linda Nell Evans
Lissa Dunlay
Mary Cline
Maynard Thomson
Michael Reklis
Mike Kaminsky
Mokhtar Ramadan
Nikki Gibson
Richard Meyer
Suejean Kim
Susan Carp
Tim Perttula

SUBSCRIBERS

Adam Hetherington
Alan Shockley
Amanda Freitag
Andrew Lemon
Andrew Strickland
Angela Kennedy
Anonymous
Antonia Lloyd-Jones
Ariel Saldivar
Balthazar Simões
Barbara Graettinger
Ben Fountain
Ben Nichols
Betsy Morrison
Bill Fisher
Bjorn Beer
Bob & Mona Ball
Bradford Pearson
Brandon Kennedy
Brina Palencia
Charles Dee Mitchell
Cheryl Thompson
Chris Sweet
Christie Tull
Clint Harbour
Daniel Hahn
Darius Frasure
David Bristow
David Hopkins
David Lowery
David Shook
Dennis Humphries
Don & Donna Goertz
Ed Nawotka
Elizabeth Caplice
Erin Baker
Ethan Segal
Fiona Schlachter
Frank Merlino
George Henson
Gino Palencia
Grace Kenney
Greg McConeghy
Horatiu Matei
Jacob Siefring
Jacob Silverman
Jacobo Luna
James Crates
Jamie Richards
Jane Owen
Jane Watson
Jeanne Milazzo
Jeff Whittington
Jennifer Smart
Jeremy Hughes
Joe Milazzo
Joel Garza
John Harvell
Joshua Edwin
Julia Pashin
Justin Childress
Kaleigh Emerson
Katherine McGuire
Kimberly Alexander
Krista Nightengale
Laura Tamayo
Lauren Shekari
Linda Nell Evans
Lissa Dunlay
Lytton Smith
Mac Tull
Marcia Lynx Qualey
Margaret Terwey
Mari Mattingly
Mark Larson
Martha Gifford
Mary Ann Thompson-Frenk & Joshua Frenk
Matthew Rowe
Meaghan Corwin
Michael Holtmann
Mike Kaminsky
Naomi Firestone-Teeter
Neal Chuang
Nick Oxford
Nikki Gibson
Norma Pace
Patrick Brown
Peter McCambridge
Regina Imburgia
Shelby Vincent
Scot Roberts
Steven Norton
Susan B. Reese
Tess Lewis
Tim Kindseth
Todd Mostrog
Tom Bowden
Tony Fleo
Wendy Walker
Weston Monroe
Will Morrison

ALSO PUBLISHED IN ENGLISH BY MIKHAIL SHISHKIN:

Maidenhair
(translated by Marian Schwartz)

The Light and the Dark
(translated by Andrew Bromfield)